A TASTE OF DANGER

SUBPARHEROES

MORGAN BRICE

eBook ISBN: 978-1-64795-071-2
Print ISBN: 978-1-64795-072-9

CONTENTS

A TASTE OF DANGER

SUBPARHEROES

By Morgan Brice

CHAPTER 1
SCOTT

"Ninety-nine, one hundred," Scott Dixon counted out loud as he checked two more failed job applications off his spreadsheet. He sighed and took a drink of his now cold coffee. "Maybe one hundred and one is the charm."

Getting laid off from his job as a food reviewer for *Taste of the Rainbow* magazine, which specialized in reviewing LGBTQ-owned and friendly restaurants, was bad enough. Receiving the notice via text two weeks ago was doubly awful.

Dear Scott—

We regret to inform you that due to declining advertising revenue, your position as a full-time food reviewer has been cut. You are free to re-apply to submit work-for-hire articles on an ad hoc basis at our free-lance rate. Your keycard and network access have been deactivated. The contents of your desk and cubicle will be boxed and mailed to you. If you had personal items elsewhere, please let us know, and we will include them in the box. Please do not return to the office as you will not be permitted to enter. We wish you well in your new endeavors.

Since Scott had been in charge of hiring freelancers, he knew how their rate compared to his salary. *Even if I freelanced the whole damn magazine issue, it wouldn't pay what I've been making.* He muttered several extremely impolite descriptions of his former boss as he got up to refill his cup. "Text messaging toadie. 'Fraidy cat fucker. Anti-social asshole."

To add insult to injury, his car needed repairs, putting a dent in his emergency stash. The unexpected expense of buying a new shirt and jacket for in-person interviews drained his funds further, even though he had found them at a consignment store.

Scott cut every subscription except his e-book and inventoried his cupboards and freezer for cheap meals so he could skip grocery shopping. Despite that, and even if he picked up some other freelance gigs to tide himself over, he couldn't go more than a couple more weeks without a real job.

Scott didn't want to sleep in his car or beg friends to let him couch surf, but that possibility loomed large unless something showed up real soon. He had less than thirty dollars in his wallet, and there wasn't enough left on his credit card to pay rent.

A fast-food gig wouldn't pay the rent, and it would eat up time I could use to job hunt. He hated the idea of pawning any of his gaming equipment—that was a last resort.

His phone rang, and he didn't recognize the number. "Hello?"

"Scott Dixon? This is April from SPAM. We received your resume and are very impressed. I'm calling to offer you a full-time, salaried position with very generous health benefits and paid vacation. We'd like you to start immediately, and there's a signing bonus to ease your relocation to Albany." She named the salary and bonus. Scott nearly swooned at the amount, a hefty upgrade from his most recent salary.

"SPAM?" Scott's mind whirled, trying to remember if he had sent a resume to Hormel. Even if he hadn't, he had heard good things, and the offer had everything he needed. "Albany? I mean, yes, thank you. Sure. I just need to pack. Thank you."

"How quickly can you come for orientation? We have a

project we'd like you to head, and it needs someone to take over in a few weeks."

"I can be in Albany in two days, just need to wrap up some things here in Rochester." Scott was still reeling from the sudden reversal of fortune. "Can you please send me something in writing?" he remembered to ask, wary because he had heard about hiring scams.

"Of course," April said. "I'll have a confirmation letter out to you this afternoon. Congratulations, and welcome to SPAM."

Scott stared at his phone for a few minutes after April hung up. *I have a job—and a raise. I'm moving to Albany. Holy shit—I've got a job!*

Only then did he realize that in his panic to keep his head above water, he had asked almost no questions—working hours, whether he had an office, how much vacation, and all the other things that he would have normally focused on. *I'll get the details when I arrive, and if it doesn't work out at least I can keep a roof over my head while I look for something else.*

Now that he thought about it, applying to SPAM did seem familiar. He had assumed it was the test kitchen for the processed meat product and given it his best shot. Scott knew that some people had definite *opinions* about the canned ham, but it was something his grandmother cooked for him when he stayed over, decorated with a slice of pineapple, which seemed exotic when he was a child.

Scott realized he didn't just *remember* the dish—he could taste it clearly in his mouth, as if he had just taken a bite, not as a long-ago memory.

Scott got an unusual taste in his mouth that tied into something unexpected happening in his life more and more often lately. He had a strong tang of soap right before his washer overflowed last week. Before that, it had been the grit of ashes seconds before a pan on his stove caught fire. And then there was the time soy sauce completely overwhelmed his taste buds minutes before a semi packed with ramen noodles overturned on the highway in front of him, blocking both lanes.

At first, Scott had chalked it all up to a twisted cosmic sense of humor or pure coincidence. But as the incidents happened more often—random, unpredictable, but never wrong—he started to wonder if there was more to them than he originally thought.

He had mentioned the odd tastes to a couple of people, who agreed it was strange but didn't have much else to add. His doctor assured him it wasn't a stroke. When it occurred with increasing frequency, always with a strange link to things that hadn't happened yet, Scott wondered if his mind was playing tricks on him.

Then he looked it up and learned a new word—clairgustance, the ability to taste something that wasn't present. Scott had stayed up late reading articles that explained clairgustance as a psychic ability, being alerted to something unknown or yet to come through the sense of taste.

It seemed like a strange—and largely useless—psychic power, hardly likely to help him win the lottery, but Scott had shrugged and accepted the oddity, figuring it would never come in handy.

Curious about the job offer, Scott looked up the address online but only found a nondescript building that lacked signage.

"I bet it's a test kitchen," Scott said aloud as he stood in the middle of his apartment's living room and tried to figure out how to pack. "I know I applied to a couple of those."

Maybe they're looking for ways to modernize the perception. I know they use SPAM in sushi in Hawaii. Maybe there are some new appetizers and cool snacks that could appeal to a younger audience.

Scott had always dreamed of working in a test kitchen, getting paid to invent recipes and update meals for modern tastes.

He didn't even mind the move to Albany despite Rochester's

trendy food scene. *I haven't met the right person here—maybe they'll be waiting for me in Albany.*

Being a food reviewer for a popular magazine had its perks. Scott had a generous expense account—which included cab fare so he could try wine pairings with the meals. He ate at all the new restaurants and bars that offered unique menus and wrote about his experiences. That meant that once or twice a week, he didn't have to pay for food and had classy leftovers for lunches.

He wasn't a mystery diner, so restaurants recognized him and made sure he got great service. It wasn't the same thing as being famous for real, but Scott enjoyed the perks as well as the notoriety. More than a few times, it had helped him impress a new date and gotten him laid.

Scott sighed. None of those dates had turned into anything solid, so there wasn't anyone to consider when he made plans to move to Albany. At thirty, Scott was ready to meet his forever guy. He'd thrown himself into Rochester's dating scene and concluded Mr. Right wasn't in this ZIP code.

People in Albany need to stay warm. That's more fun with two. Scott wasn't a hardcore outdoor enthusiast, and he preferred fireplaces to ski slopes, but he could think of plenty of pleasant ways to spend a cold day with a hot partner.

"If I don't find someone after a reasonable time, I can always move," he told himself as he figured out how many boxes he needed to pack up his things. *Please let me find someone.*

Scott eyed the magazines piled on his bookshelf, each with one of his reviews. He had intended to make a portfolio but hadn't taken the time.

Maybe that's because I never really intended to be a food reviewer as a permanent gig.

When he had gone to culinary school, Scott wanted to open a trendy tapas restaurant with an extensive and quirky wine list, regional hard ciders and meads, and small-batch, locally brewed beers.

He hadn't given up on that dream, but Scott quickly learned

how much capital he'd need to make that a reality. He had tested the concept with rented food trucks and carts and found it went over great with tourists and young professionals. But he hadn't been able to get a loan or find a partner he trusted—in business or personal ways—so Scott put the dream on hold.

The new job pays more. I could save up quicker. An online search reassured him that Albany had a small but energetic foodie scene. To the north, in the Adirondack region, plenty of lodges and ski towns catered to tourists who didn't all want to rough it while they explored the great outdoors.

This could work. Get to know the area, meet the food notables through SPAM, maybe find investors, or get a chef's position where I can do innovative small bites.

Since his childhood dream of becoming a superhero hadn't panned out, Scott swore he would cling to his vision of shaking up the culinary world.

Back in the day, he daydreamed about being a chef who could use magic to make food that changed villains into good guys and brought warring factions to world peace. A few years in the reality of a busy commercial kitchen under temperamental chefs with a penchant for throwing meat cleavers led him to believe peace on earth would have to find a different route.

Then he developed his odd ability to predict the future by the taste in his mouth and occasionally imagined himself stopping spies from poisoning world leaders or deactivating a hidden bomb in the nick of time.

Since he'd gotten the reviewing job, putting him in the dining room instead of the kitchen, he had stopped imagining heroic exploits. His superhero alter-ego got put on the shelf along with his aspirations. *I hung up my cape when I picked up an apron.*

I might not get to be a superhero—predicting the future because I've got a funny taste in my mouth isn't going to be the stuff of a blockbuster movie. But maybe I can reclaim my dreams and quit being a chump.

Scott walked around his apartment, figuring how to pack up

his DVDs, video games, books, and electronics, as well as his keepsakes and souvenirs. The furniture belonged to the apartment, but he had nice linens and lots of chef-quality cooking equipment that he intended to take with him.

He looked at his shelf of customized pop culture figurines with big heads who looked like the hosts from that English baking show and who had become his erstwhile sounding board.

"You're going to be proud of me," he told them. "Maybe I'll come up with some great new recipes worthy of a handshake. This could be the beginning of a whole new season for me."

They remained stoic and silent, as always, but Scott got the taste of fig jam, which he took as approval.

I've been marking time, spinning my wheels as a food reviewer. I should have gotten into a test kitchen ages ago and seen what I could do. Maybe I'll fall on my face—but at least I'll know.

Scott packed up his apartment, paid the cleaning fee, rented a truck with a tow hitch for his Honda Pilot, and headed for Albany. When he realized that other than giving notice to his landlord and the magazine, he didn't really have anyone to say goodbye to, Scott felt even more sure he'd made the right decision.

The taste of chocolate chip cookies out of nowhere seemed to confirm that choice.

Scott turned the music up as he drove and tried to enjoy the scenery. Albany was not far from the Adirondacks, an area Scott had always wanted to explore. *There are a lot of classy lodges and hotels in the mountains. Maybe we can get our test kitchen food into them.*

Scott realized that he had never lost his fascination with creating new recipes and testing them out, which he had gained as a culinary student and in his first few jobs with edgy, experimental restaurants. He wished he had parlayed that into more of the articles he wrote. But the editor wanted to highlight food and restaurants that would appeal to a broader audience, so cutting edge got replaced with expensive but predictable. *Maybe getting fired will turn out to be the best thing that's ever happened to me. Now if I can just meet my forever guy while I'm cooking up a storm.*

He turned up the volume louder on a favorite song and reached for his soda as he drove, trying to remember the last time he had been on a date. *I was writing the review on that new taco-barbeque place, because we went there together. The food wasn't good and the date fizzled.*

After that, Scott kept himself so busy with article assignments for the magazine and expanded features for the website and social media pages that he had plenty of excuses for not going out on dates.

I went out to restaurants every week. Weekends were when I stayed home and enjoyed some peace and quiet. It was a good enough excuse to stop friends from pushing, but Scott knew he was dodging the issue.

This time last year, Scott thought his boyfriend Benji might be the one after he jumped back into the dating pool. They enjoyed going out to clubs, but they also had a good time with a quiet evening at home, which Scott actually preferred. One day, he came home to find Benji's things packed in a moving van and learned he had only been a bed warmer until Benji found a better partner who could advance his career.

Devastated, Scott had again retreated into his work, only socializing with a few close friends and staying away from the clubs. Lately, he thought about putting himself out there, seeing if he could find someone special, but hadn't found the nerve.

There hasn't been anyone since Benji. I need to let go of that and move on. Maybe a change of luck will come with a change of scenery. This is exactly what I need: new town, fresh start, different job. Maybe I'll meet someone who isn't an asshole. Go back to creating recipes. Take a chance on a food truck. At least I can say I tried.

April from SPAM sent him the address for a temporary apartment they had rented for him until he could get his bearings. Two months of corporate-paid housing was included in the surprisingly generous relocation package April had emailed to him.

He couldn't stay there permanently since the unit was owned by the company and used for new hires and short-term consultants, but it saved him from moving into a hotel and then having to move again. And if they planned to send him out on assignment right after his training, like the phone call suggested, it meant he didn't have to worry about signing a lease of his own until he came back to Albany.

For now, Scott had a roof over his head and somewhere to dump his stuff while he met his new boss and got a feel for the requirements of the job. Once he knew more about where he would be working and what hours were expected—and got the lay of the land—he intended to look for a comfortable apartment of his own and check out the Albany social scene.

I needed a shakeup to get off my ass and start over. This is a stretch—and I haven't had a real challenge in a long time. I think this could be the perfect way to start over.

Scott pulled into the apartment building and sat for a moment after he parked, getting a grip on how fast his life had changed. Capital Suites looked respectable enough that Scott wasn't worried about having his car stolen. The sudden taste of strawberries—his favorite—seemed to confirm that he would be safe here. The taste cues came more often recently, and Scott realized that he now automatically weighed them into his decision-making, which oddly, didn't seem strange at all.

Very literally a sixth sense. Let's just hope warnings of bad stuff don't taste like garbage or poop.

Scott picked up the key at the rental office front desk after showing his ID. The apartment SPAM set up for him was more like a hotel suite, which sounded fancier than the reality. That just meant instead of just a bedroom and bathroom, he had a small kitchenette, dining table, and a couch facing the TV. *I guess it qualifies as an efficiency, maybe?* he thought. Still, if it took a while to find an apartment it beat sitting on the bed for everything.

He hadn't taken any time to search for a place to live, figuring it could wait until he could drive around Albany and see the city for himself. Scott hoped that SPAM would have relocation advice or perhaps arrangements with local apartment complexes for an employee discount. At the very least, he figured he could talk to some other people working at SPAM and get tips on everything from places to live to dry cleaners.

Scott left his knickknacks boxed and his artwork bubble-wrapped, focused on moving everything valuable or immediately necessary out of the rented moving trailer so he could return it before they charged him for another day. It depressed him that at this point in life, everything he owned fit in his SUV and a small trailer. He stacked the boxes of things he wouldn't need right away against the apartment wall, figuring he could live out of suitcases until he got through orientation and his first assignment.

Once he had taken care of returning the trailer, it was nearly dinnertime. Scott spotted a deli that rated well and took home the most luscious Reuben he had ever seen, along with chips, pickle spears, and a bottle of soda. He breathed a sigh of relief when nothing in his apartment had been touched and spread out the butcher paper to feast on his sandwich.

This time, the taste of pickle and spicy mustard was anticipation, not a premonition.

After he finished dinner—and resolved to remember the name of the deli—Scott fired up his laptop.

He had read all about the history of canned meat and the company that made it, the market trends and popular perception, and scanned recipes. Now, he put in the address that April supplied in his welcome email along with half a dozen forms to complete and did a search so he knew where to go in the morning.

"Huh." The building didn't have any markings to suggest a relationship with the canned ham or its maker. The unremarkable, four-story building didn't look like the kind of place for a commercial kitchen. If he had driven past it, Scott would have guessed it housed insurance agencies and white-collar offices for law firms or financial organizations.

He tried the search a couple of ways after checking April's email and always got the same results. Since it was after hours, Scott decided to wait until morning to call so he could check directions and verify the address.

Oddly enough, neither the ham nor its company showed up as having any past or current presence in Albany. He checked for corporate partners, thinking the facility might be under another company name, and found nothing.

"Strange," he muttered. He searched on test kitchens and found three cooking schools and a mobile caterer.

Would they have a secret location? Maybe they're working on a major rebrand or pivoting their marketing direction and want to keep it quiet. That must be it. This is even more exciting than I thought.

Over the last two days, Scott had looked up what to expect from his new city. Albany had a reputation for coffee shops, fish fry, and cheesecake, as well as a local specialty known as Melba sauce. Thanks to several nearby colleges, music festivals, winter sports, and live theater provided plenty of things to do, and farmers' markets were a hot ticket in good weather. Historic locations drew scholars and tourists since Albany was the state capital.

Even better, Albany rated as gay friendly and offered local organizations, bars, restaurants, and events that made getting to know people and finding community easier. Scott looked forward to exploring and hoped the city was as welcoming as its Chamber of Commerce promised.

Scott had already filled out some initial paperwork online,

enough to get his direct deposit and health insurance set up. More documents surprised him, but he dug in hoping to make his first day go smoother.

Have you ever fomented revolution in a foreign country?
No.

Are you now, or have you ever been, on a watch list for revolutionaries?
No.

Have you ever been renditioned? If so, please explain.
No.

Have you died and been brought back to life more than once?
No.

Scott checked to make sure he hadn't opened some sort of joke form by accident. *They either have a really strange sense of humor or an exceptionally thorough human resources department.*

Please list any personal experience with Weapons of Mass Destruction. Be sure to include poisons (solid, gas, liquid) and radioactive materials.

He quickly put N/A.

If you have attracted the ire of any covens, nests, or packs, please provide details.

Scott stared at the question for a moment. *This is a joke, right? They want to see how well I react to strange situations. I can show them I go with the flow.* Another N/A.

Please list any unusual abilities. If you have come to the attention of any governmental organization, public or secret, please make a note.

What the fuck?

Scott thought about his clairgustance and decided that was too odd. He certainly hadn't attracted attention from any spy organizations. *Would I know if I had?* Erring on the side of caution, he mentioned the ability, but downplayed it. *That should cover my ass.*

Do you have any unusual allergies (sensitivity to silver, holy water, or salt, for example) that we should know about?

Scott generally thought he had a good sense of humor, but this was starting to weird him out.

None—not even garlic, he wrote, then backspaced over the last three words.

Do you require any special shielding materials to be in place to protect others' safety or privacy from your talents?

Scott couldn't help snickering like a twelve year-old. *Regular condoms work just fine,* he thought, but marked N/A.

Please name your next of kin, memorial service religious preferences (if any), and any dangers inherent in burial or cremation. If an alternative disposal is required, please note how and why.

Scott sat back and stared at the form. "Next of kin? Alternative disposal? Are they expecting me to fall in a radioactive frying vat?"

He filled out the answers, feeling sad that the best he could do for his next of kin was his sister, who like the rest of his family, was estranged after he came out. *Julie might at least make arrangements long-distance. That's the best I've got.*

Any personal weapons brought onto the premises remain the responsibility of the owner. SPAM will not be responsible for damages or discharge.

I've been in plenty of hot kitchens, but never with anyone packing heat. Except for that one guy, Gino, at the pizza place in college. I'm still pretty sure he was delivering weed with the pizzas.

The stereotype of diva chefs with quick tempers exists for a reason. Letting them bring weapons doesn't seem like a good idea. Maybe the test kitchen is in a bad part of town, but it didn't look like it from the maps.

He had thought it odd that the SPAM headquarters hadn't shown up on the satellite photos as if something obscured the building from view. *Maybe there are power lines overhead. That can mess up images. Weird.*

Scott finished the questionnaire and started on the medical form. It seemed more normal, although the allergy question came up again. Some questions made him give the laptop a boggled look.

Do you heal exceptionally fast or slow? Please explain.

That wasn't too weird.

In the event that you are unconscious, do you require extra sedation to keep your abilities under control?

Like I'm going to sing karaoke or something? He marked No.

What is your kryptonite?

Scott had heard personal development trainers ask that question—metaphorically—but had never experienced it on a health questionnaire. *Green chiles and andouille sausage give me indigestion,* he finally wrote.

The rest of the form was fairly normal, and Scott wondered whether the strange questions were some sort of personality test to see how well he adapted to unexpected conditions. That seemed like a very avant-garde hiring approach for a test kitchen but figured maybe they were checking his inherent creativity.

Scott hit send and sat back with a relieved sigh. Paperwork was always the worst part of any job. He poured himself a couple of fingers of whiskey and realized that he had to unpack at least some of his clothes and necessities before he could go to bed.

Just for a moment, it struck him that he was alone in a city where he knew no one, living in a temporary apartment, far away from people who, if not his besties, knew him and were willing to lend a hand.

Did I do the right thing taking this job? I jumped at it because I was desperate, but I've uprooted my whole life after one phone conversation.

What if I don't like the people? What if the work isn't satisfying? How long will it take me to get to know my co-workers? And will I finally meet someone who can be more than just a weekend fling?

Worst case, I don't last and end up freelancing for the magazine and seeing if I can pick up enough other gigs to keep body and soul together. I'll find a way to make it work—somehow.

Scott had sent emails to the work colleagues he liked to let them know he had found a new job and was moving. Since his phone number and email address wouldn't change, they didn't need a street address if they wanted to keep in touch. Their friendship had been largely based on proximity, so he wondered how many of them would bother.

He didn't need a large circle of friends, but Scott liked to hang out with people who shared the same interests in movies, shows, books, and games. There had been a couple of friends who enjoyed going to the same sort of movies or playing role-playing games. Scott knew he would miss them. But given how long he had lived in Rochester, it didn't seem like he had left much of a footprint, which made him sad.

Spending time with people without anything in common took too much effort, and he didn't care about gossip or personal drama.

Scott didn't have any trouble starting a conversation when he spotted shared interests, including food. He often daydreamed about what Mr. Right would look like for him and had concluded his perfect match would probably be doing something food-related.

I'm tired of sleeping alone—and not just for sex. I want to come home to someone who loves me, someone who intends to stick around. Someone who will always be there for me, and we can protect each other.

He didn't intend to get drunk the night before starting a new job, but all alone in a strange place, Scott wanted to take the edge off the loneliness.

The television carried enough channels for him to find a rerun of a favorite show and binge-watch a couple of episodes until the whiskey kicked in. Despite the alcohol, his mind still raced.

Maybe I should get a dog. It's certainly not a substitute for meeting the right guy, but at least I wouldn't feel quite as alone.

They say dogs are a great way to meet people. I could take him on walks, go to dog parks, and meet cute guys.

I should look at rescues once I get settled. Maybe we can give each other a fresh start.

Scott's family had different types of dogs when he was growing up. His mom went through a small dog phase with Pomeranians and Pekingese, while his dad picked Labradors and German shepherds. Other family members had beagles and golden retrievers, poodles and mutts, and one infamous Yorkie who chased Scott's grandfather up a tree.

Out of all of them, Scott's favorites were the big dogs. He liked being able to tussle and appreciated their stamina for long walks and games of fetch. Many people were wary of guard dogs like shepherds, but Scott saw their goofy side and thought they were endearing.

Something to look forward to, he thought, and realized how much he had missed having a dog around. His last dog, a marvelous mixed breed named Flynn, had died of old age a year ago, and Scott had been so off-kilter from the changing environment at the magazine that he had postponed looking for a new companion until things settled down.

Anticipating finding a furry friend cheered him, lifting his heavy mood. *This move might just turn out to be the right thing after all.*

CHAPTER 2
SCOTT

Scott tried to quell his nervousness while he got ready to go to the office.

April's email had said business casual, so Scott picked a burgundy shirt over black pants, hoping it looked slightly dressy while not being a suit. He made sure to eat breakfast before he changed so that his nervousness didn't make him spill food or coffee on his shirt.

They've already hired me. It's not an interview—I'm meeting the team and going to orientation. Somehow, that didn't make him feel any less fidgety.

When he drove to the headquarters, his map app glitched, so he ended up driving past a couple of times before he spotted the street number above the door. *I hope they got a discount on the rent if they've got that much electromagnetic interference. They should take that up with the landlord. Should I be worried about growing a tumor or a second head? Beggars can't be choosers. Make some money, sock it away, and quit before I turn into a radioactive creature.*

Scott parked and took a few deep breaths before heading inside. A bored receptionist glanced up when he entered.

"I'm Scott Dixon, the new hire. April told me to come here for orientation."

The woman looked at him in silence, blew a bubble, and popped it. "Identification, please."

Scott hurried to produce his license. She peered at it over her glasses and handed it back. "Orientation is on the first floor. You'll need an escort until they've done your paperwork and issued you an ID."

The receptionist slid a laminated, clip-on badge across the counter. It read "GUEST—Zero Clearance, Escort Required."

"You've got pretty tight security," Scott observed and figured perhaps the competitiveness of developing new snack foods or recipes warranted extra caution.

She smacked her gum. "Goes with the territory. You don't want to see what happens without it."

"I suspect you're right."

"Trust me, you don't. Last time, heads rolled. It was not a pretty sight."

Scott knew the restaurant business could be highly competitive. Rochester had an active foodie scene, but he hadn't heard that Albany—generally regarded as a sleepy town despite being the state capital—had such a cut-throat reputation.

"Have a seat." She nodded toward a gray bench along the wall. "Your escort will be here to take you inside."

Scott sat and tried not to fidget. He thought about reading the news or playing a game on his phone but didn't want to appear distracted. Instead, he looked around and was confused by the completely neutral lobby, devoid of any connection to canned ham or other food products. Two of the most generic landscape paintings Scott had ever seen broke up the expanse of light gray walls. He didn't catch any whiff of cooking smells. No company logos or corporate pictures hung on the walls, but Scott spotted a security camera pointed at the main doorway and a small sliding door that made him think, bizarrely, of a sniper's roost.

A man in military fatigues came out of a door at the back of the lobby and looked around.

"Scott Dixon?"

Feeling even more confused, Scott stood. "Hi. I'm the new hire—test kitchen."

The man looked to be in his early forties, with a high-and-tight haircut and the bearing of a career soldier. "You're the new guy. Welcome. I'm Ted. April said to expect you. I'm here to show you around, help you get your bearings, and get your equipment issued."

"Okay." Scott was utterly confused but doing his best to go with the flow.

Ted led him down the hallway and stopped at a door marked "Armory."

"Do you have a preference in manufacturer or caliber?"

"In what?"

Ted opened the door and ushered Scott into a room whose walls were covered in guns. Handguns, semi-automatics, rifles, shotguns—and quite a few Scott couldn't even identify.

"I don't understand."

"If you brought your own pieces, they need to be registered with the organization," Ted went on as if he hadn't heard. "You'll get a service handgun, regular issue, and you can request a long gun or automatic if you want."

"I—"

"Well? These are all standard models." Ted seemed to expect Scott to know his way around guns.

"That one." At a loss, Scott pointed to one that looked impressive.

"Glock. Good choice. We'll get you a shoulder holster that fits. Any other guns?"

A very long time ago, Scott's grandfather had taken him out hunting groundhogs. "Double-barrel shotgun?" he asked, completely flummoxed.

Ted nodded. "Good general-purpose weapon. You can always request something else if you have a situation that requires it. We'll handle the paperwork and have them ready to take with you."

Ted headed to a different area in the armory which had the kind of tactical vests Scott had seen in action movies. "Step over here, and we'll get you fitted."

Scott followed in a daze, and a man with a measuring tape stepped up, reminding him of the last time he had bought a suit. "Isn't this a little overkill?" Scott managed.

Ted fixed him with a look. "This is a dangerous business. We can't be too careful."

Scott wracked his memories to see if he could recall anyone at a test kitchen being shot or blown up. Even the cooking competitions didn't go that far.

Ted went to a set of shelves and searched for what looked like a black leather dopp kit. "This has everything you'll need—lockpicks, micro-bugs, an earpiece, micro camera, night vision monocular, bug detectors, and a shiv, just in case."

Scott started to hyperventilate. "Hold up—"

"Sorry, we're on a very tight schedule."

"Wait a fucking minute!" Scott burst out. "I got hired to be a chef in a test kitchen. I'm not James Bond."

Ted gave a slow blink. "Test kitchen?"

"Yes. For canned meat products. Cooking appetizers and casseroles and creating lunch ideas." Scott felt a little light-headed. "Putting canned ham back on top. The all-American processed meat. You know—SPAM."

Ted looked at him as if Scott had two heads. "April hired you."

"Yes."

"She processed your paperwork."

"Yes, and she set things up for me to come here today to start my new job. As a test kitchen chef."

Ted's nonplussed expression made Scott grit his teeth. "Did April actually use the term test kitchen?"

Now that he thought about it, Scott wasn't sure. But it had seemed so at the time. "I—she said I had just what the organization needed. And she was very interested in my little psychic thing."

"Your little psychic thing?"

Scott was getting pretty pissed at Ted for repeating him. "Yes. The whole weird thing where I get a taste in my mouth, and something related happens."

"Clairgustance. That would be why you were recruited. Handy for an agent," Ted replied.

If it was making sense for him, it was clear as mud for Scott. "I'm not an agent. I'm a food reviewer. I cook. I want to have a food truck someday. I really think you've got the wrong man." His eyes widened, and he went pale with fear. "Oh, God. Does that mean you have to kill me now?"

"Probably not." Ted was entirely too calm for the situation. "I need to speak to someone."

"Fuck—that's why you had me fill out next of kin. You're going to kill me and harvest my organs. Or traffic me. How about if I go back to Rochester, and we just forget any of this ever happened?"

Ted gave him a pitying look. "I'm afraid I can't do that, Scott."

Scott didn't realize he had been backing up until he hit the wall. "That's what the computer in that movie said right before it tried to kill everyone."

Ted took a step closer, moving slowly as if approaching a wild animal. "Didn't April tell you this is the Special Processing And Management division? Aka SPAM. We handle unique covert intelligence operations that involve the supernatural and paranormal abilities."

"Covert intelligence? You mean I'm a spy?"

Ted shrugged. "That's very Cold War. We prefer intelligence asset or operative. Gotta keep up with the times."

"Why would anyone recruit me to be a spy?" Scott figured he would ask questions now so that if they shot him once he fainted, he would at least die with answers.

"You applied for the job. Your qualifications were outstanding."

"I applied to be a chef in a test kitchen. The application didn't say anything about killing people, infiltrating foreign governments, assassinating politicians, or blowing up secret bunkers."

Ted looked a little hurt. "There are many hurtful stereotypes. That's why we have orientation."

Scott began to pace. "Oh, God. Shit. Fuck. Damn. I gave up my apartment, moved to Albany, and now I'm a spy." He looked at Ted. "Do you at least have a division that infiltrates fancy government parties? I could be good at that. I could be a fake waiter and wear a microphone. Maybe I could fix the appetizers for secret meetings. You have to eat well when you're planning sneaky stuff to save the world."

Ted touched a button on his collar. "April?"

April's voice sounded through the small button-speaker. "Is Scott with you?"

"He's very confused—something about being hired for a test kitchen?"

She chuckled. "That sort of thing happens. Hello, Scott."

"Please don't kill me. I'll forget everything. Swear I won't tell a soul."

"Calm down, Scott," she replied. "We have a slight misunderstanding."

"You think?" Scott began to pace in earnest. "All I wanted was to get a job making delicious food so I could show those bastards at the magazine I was a good chef and make a living doing what I love. And now they're giving me guns and body armor and listening devices that I'm pretty sure are illegal in all fifty states and territories, and Ted says I'm a spy now, and that means people are going to shoot me, and I'll never get my food truck." Scott wasn't sure whether he was more likely to pass out or throw up.

"Please don't be alarmed," April said, in a voice that sounded way too close to the monotone of automated messages to give Scott any real comfort. "Let's take things one step at a time."

"Let's start with the spy stuff. I thought you worked for the company that makes canned ham."

April laughed. "We get that a lot. We're really way cooler. We're actually Special Processing And Management, and we handle spying with agents who have unusual and technically small—but definitely not insignificant—paranormal abilities. Offbeat powers, like yours."

"I get funny tastes in my mouth. I'm not going to save the world with that," Scott countered.

"You never know." April grew serious. "Much stranger things have happened. But unconventional abilities aren't as likely to be spotted. Some of the supes practically *glow* with how much power they have—hard to go unnoticed. You, on the other hand—"

"I'm a chef!"

"And that's exactly what we need for the assignment we're giving you. Someone is creating dangerous recreational drugs and distilled spirits specifically altered to affect creatures with supernatural metabolisms," April went on as if her statement held nothing unusual. "Bootleggers and smugglers. They're black market, unregulated, untested—and unsafe. We need someone with your background to find out where the altered materials are coming from and help us shut down the suppliers."

Scott frowned, trying to figure out the goal. "Is it illegal to make recipes for special metabolisms?"

"Not technically—although we've raised issues with the powers that be about the potential problems," she replied. "Faster metabolisms burn off any kind of substance faster than normal, and it takes more to affect them. As long as no one is getting hurt, we've turned a blind eye. We're not interested in the legitimate makers, at least not until there are regulations in place. The big issue is that what's coming in from Canada is tainted, and there have been deaths."

"When you say creatures with supernatural metabolisms," Scott said, feeling like his head was full of wool, "you mean—"

"Vampires, shifters, werewolves, and some of the less common creatures," April answered matter-of-factly.

"They're real?"

"Oh, yes. One of our mandates is to keep the supernatural community safe from entities that would try to harm or exploit them," April told him.

"Entities…"

"I know this is all new to you," she said, "but that's why there's orientation. We recruit people from all walks of life who have the talent to help us accomplish our missions. And if you recall, the terms of our package are very competitive—generous, even."

They gave me a raise and a bonus. Healthcare. Funeral expenses. It's a better package than anything else I saw available. I gave up my apartment and moved here. I don't have enough money to keep looking.

"Okay." Scott surrendered to fate. "What do I need to do?"

"That's the spirit," April cheered. "It's a lot to take in all at once, but after you've gone through orientation and we get you on your first assignment, you'll get the hang of it. I know you're going to do great. Gotta run. Stay in touch!"

The link went quiet, and Scott stared at Ted. He felt as if his world had come unstuck. Sure, when he was a kid he thought it would be cool to be a spy like in the movies and comic books. Then he read some John Le Carre novels and decided the danger, solitude, deception, betrayals, and loneliness weren't something he was cut out for.

"Here's your orientation schedule," Ted replied, in a tone as if the whole conversation hadn't happened. "It starts off with a cocktail hour, first names only. Look for chemistry with possible partners, but remember that allegiances shift and loyalties change, so don't get too attached.

"Next, you have the kick-off dinner with a speech by the head of SPAM about our history and mission. There's a film afterward about the organization's history—the part that isn't classified, anyhow.

"Oh, and wear these at all times." Ted pulled a small bag from his pocket and handed it to Scott. Inside were two silver charms on silver chains. The designs looked like ancient sigils. Scott slipped the necklaces over his head and tucked them beneath his shirt.

"Tomorrow, we'll assess your gun knowledge and teach you some basic self-defense moves. Then we have several presentations: Interrogation Under Torture—Just Say Nyet, Ten Ways to Recognize Other Spies, and My Cover is Blown—Now What?" Ted paused.

"You'll also get an official physical, and we'll issue your badge along with a wallet card on who to contact if you need to be extracted in an emergency. You'll have basic hand-to-hand combat and weapons training before being debriefed on your assignment and released to the field." Ted concluded.

Scott felt like he might have a case of the vapors. "I don't know how to fight. The last guy I hit was Auggie Andrews in the fifth grade because he stuck my math book in the toilet. And I'm gay. You're not allowed to have gay spies, right?"

Ted sighed. "Did you ever, for even a minute, think James Bond *didn't* swing both ways?"

Believe me, that crossed my mind. Scott had plenty of fantasies about peeling that tuxedo off more than one incarnation of the famous spy. "I'm not accustomed to danger."

"You were a food critic. Surely you had enemies."

Scott thought for a moment. "There was a chef with a meat cleaver who didn't like what I said about his béarnaise sauce. But since they all wanted positive reviews, they mostly sucked up to me. It was nice while it lasted."

"We won't be sending you into combat," Ted promised. "Actually, your background as a food critic will be a perfect cover. If it helps, think of yourself as an investigator. You'll have a reason to go to the restaurants and bars we think are operating as a front for the smugglers. Some of those groups are also bringing in similarly augmented, off-the-books paranormal pharmaceuticals, so you may end up bagging some big-wigs."

Scott frowned. "How are they getting the supplies?"

"They're a bunch of coyotes coming in from Canada," Ted said.

"I thought coyotes brought undocumented people across the border," Scott replied.

Ted shook his head. "Not those kind. The furry sort—shifters."

"Real coyotes…running illegal drugs." Scott's world tilted again. "Isn't that more a problem for a game warden?"

"You've got the perfect background as a food reviewer to get into the locations and ask lots of questions. Poke around. Talk to people. Keep your eyes open. The restaurants and bars they're operating out of want good publicity. Half the time, the front of the house has no idea what's going on in the back of the kitchen," Ted assured him, ignoring his question.

If I go back to Rochester now, I'll be sleeping on couches and sending more resumes. I'm overqualified for fast food and underqualified for haute cuisine. I don't want to be broke. Scott slumped in surrender. "Okay. I'll do it."

Ted smiled. "You'll be a natural. Your cover is as a food writer. We aren't expecting you to go in guns blazing. You get cozy with them for your article. Keep your eyes and ears open. And when you know who's who and what's where, you phone it in, and our team swoops in like the wrath of God and shuts them down."

Scott just stared at him. "And you don't think they'll figure I ratted them out and come after me?"

"We'll extract you before the team goes in," Ted assured him. "We take very good care of our assets."

I'm an asset. A spy. And I didn't even get a secret decoder ring.

"Aren't there a bunch of other things I need to know?" Scott tried to remember every espionage movie he had ever seen. "Like how to hotwire a car or make a bomb out of household materials or defuse a nuke with a paperclip?"

"Those skills are strictly on a need-to-know basis," Ted replied. "If you're ever assigned a case where it's likely you will need to do any of those things, instruction will be provided."

I wanted him to laugh and tell me that was completely nonsense. But no—it's just that I'm too junior to know how to blow things up. He took a couple of deep breaths and tried to remind himself that real spies didn't faint. "Where am I supposed to find these bootleggers?"

"We're sending you to Fox Hollow. It's a little town in between Lake Placid and Lake George. Pretty close to the Canadian border. There's an institute for psychics there, and the town itself is shifter-friendly," Ted replied. "That will all be covered as part of your assignment debrief, and they'll also give you more information about shifters and the supernatural community so you know what to look for."

"What the hell is 'shifter friendly'?"

Ted's smile looked strained. "The year-round residents tend to be either psychics or shifters. We don't think townspeople are involved in the smuggling—not knowingly, at least. That'll be part of your job—finding out whether the smugglers have inside connections."

The name of the town sounded familiar. *Didn't one of my profs from Ithaca move there? He might be able to help.*

"What if the coyotes find out I'm a spy?"

Ted's expression grew sober. "That would be very bad. Try not to let that happen."

CHAPTER 3
GAGE

Two wolves, a fox, a lynx, and a large police dog emerged from the forest, loping across the distance between the treeline and the house. They headed for a small shelter where they chose changing stalls and emerged human and fully clothed.

"That was a great run." Gage Merrick grinned broadly at his friends, Russ and Drew Lowe, Liam Reynard, and Noah Wilson.

"It's a good temperature." Liam smoothed a hand through his red hair. It wasn't difficult to imagine him as a fox. "And not too humid. I get frizzy when it's humid."

Russ and Liam were a mated pair, as were Drew and Noah. Russ looked at his mate with long-suffering affection. "Have I mentioned lately that you're a diva?"

Liam returned a dramatic stare. "Of course I am, dah-ling. That's one of the many things you love about me."

That was fun. We should run more often. I like our pack, Gage's inner Malinois said, sounding relaxed after the exercise.

I'm not sure we're a pack, Gage silently protested.

We run together. We would protect each other. We are friends. Two mated pairs and us. We need a mate so that we match, his dog side replied.

You just want to get laid.

His Malinois shrugged its elegant black and tan shoulders. *Of course. So do you. There was that guy—*

He's ancient history.

Not so very long ago.

Not long enough. Gage's academic record was top-notch. His dating record, on the other hand, was a series of strikes and misses. While he didn't have trouble getting dates, finding anyone who wanted to do more than party seemed a lost cause. His most recent misadventure ended when his boyfriend developed a chronic allergy to dogs and sneezed whenever Gage was in the room.

We are not different here. There are lots of shifters in this town. We run with the top dogs—and the little red fox, his shifter side noted with pride.

Do NOT let Liam ever hear us call him little. He's fierce. He once went batshit crazy on a poacher and practically scratched the guy's eyes out.

Commendable. We've made good friends. Much better than where we were before. I didn't get to come out as often.

Being a shifter in a city posed problems. Gage had to be careful that he didn't get picked up by the dog catcher or shot by an overzealous cop who was afraid of an unaccompanied Malinois's potential for harm.

We are impressive and handsome. A protector, his dog preened.

That was true, Gage had to admit. He didn't know how the shifters made it work when their human and animal bodies were very different sizes, but his Malinois was tall and solid, so while it wasn't exactly an even trade, he was a big, muscular dog with a reputation for law enforcement and military work that made people give him space.

We're not the big dog on the block next to the wolves.

No, but we run with them, and they respect us. Even the fox. I like this town.

Russ and Drew had dark hair like their wolves. Gage's hair

was brown with streaks of gold like his Belgian Malinois alter ego. Liam's red hair had brown undertones. Noah, the lynx, had sandy hair with some stray black strands.

Other traits remained consistent between their shifter and human sides for those who knew what to look for. The Lowe brothers were committed to family and social connections. Liam's clever, playful, and dramatic nature showed his fox. Curious and independent, Noah was the quietest of the bunch. And Gage's friendly, protective and very stubborn traits remained true to the guard dog side of his personality.

The stubborn part certainly paid off when it came to brewing craft beer, Gage's hobby, obsession, and now, his full-time job.

"Are you coming down to the brewery later? It's RPG Night," Gage said as they headed inside for coffee and bacon.

"Sounds fun. We can stop in for a while," Russ replied, and Drew nodded.

"And I need to size up the space for the reading night." Liam sipped his coffee. "Now that the weather is getting colder, people will like being inside instead of on the patio. Perfect for some readings and book talk." Liam ran the Fox Hollow library and was always looking for community engagement opportunities.

"I'm debuting a new flavor, and there will be munchies, so be sure to come early," Gage said. "I need to see how the new brew affects you."

"You always have good specialty beers," Noah said. "They're different but not too weird."

"I'll take that as a compliment," Gage laughed.

"This is where you try to get us drunk, but you give us food and get us a ride home," Liam pointed out. "I can be bought."

Shifters, like other supernatural creatures, had a higher tolerance for alcohol than regular humans. Gage had heard the same was true for both recreational and therapeutic drugs as well. That led to an underground network of medical providers for paranormals, but it also made it harder to unwind on a Saturday night.

Gage had taken it as a personal challenge to brew beers that he could actually get buzzed on. While he had no intention of enabling vampire alcoholics or drunk werewolves, it just seemed wrong that those in the paranormal community couldn't relax like their human counterparts.

"I got a little tipsy on the most recent batch," Gage said. "I'm curious to see how it works for everyone else."

"Liam's the lightweight," Russ pointed out, and Liam blew him raspberries. "We should bring Brandon."

Brandon, a moose shifter, was a regular in their friend group. While Brandon was tall and muscular as a human, Gage had no idea how much booze it would take to get a moose snockered.

"Riley could be the control in the test," Drew said. "Since he's not a shifter." Riley and Brandon were a couple.

"The more the merrier. I'll pay someone to drive you home if you get a buzz."

"If that happens, I doubt it will last long," Russ said.

"One problem at a time," Gage replied cheerily. The alarm went off on his phone.

"Speaking of which—duty calls. I'm going to head to the brewery, but come tonight if you can. And thanks for the run!"

He drove from Russ and Liam's house to the small brewery in a repurposed building at the edge of town. Gage still felt a thrill of pride when he saw the sign "Merrick Craft Brewing."

Unlike his new friends, Gage wasn't a Fox Hollow native. He had happened upon the town on a long-ago camping trip, and been surprised to discover it had a secret identity as a haven for misfit shifters and psychics.

Since Gage felt constrained about his shifting near where he lived in Schenectady, he was open to finding somewhere that would be a good place to indulge his passion for small-batch craft brew and maybe—just maybe—enable him to meet his forever person.

When he had gotten a job at the Fox Hollow Brewery over the summers during college, Gage knew he was in the right place. He came back year after year and got to know the brewery's owner. Gage's fascination with craft beer had led to a degree in brewing, which he had been pleasantly surprised to be able to pursue without leaving upstate New York.

Eventually the former owner decided to retire and offered him a sweetheart deal to purchase the business. Gage felt like the path was clear to make his dream come true. Armed with seed money from a small inheritance, a couple of beer-enthusiast investors, and a bank loan, Gage had moved to Fox Hollow, bought the brewery, and put everything he had on the line to make it successful.

For the first several months, he slept on a cot in his office. After that, he rented a room at a motel before he felt comfortable getting a real apartment and recently, a cabin of his own. Now, the brewery operated firmly in the black, and he felt certain that if he could crack the puzzle of giving creatures like himself a way to have a buzzy night on the town, the brewery would not only be on solid financial ground but set new profit records.

Sometimes the uncertainty still woke him in the middle of the night, but over the last several years, the brewery found its footing and a legion of fans. Some were from Fox Hollow and glad to support a new business. Others were campers and tourists who happened upon the brewery and took advantage of being able to ship their favorites home.

Gage headed home to get a shower before he went in to work. Bobby, his brewmaster, was already there, overseeing the second shift and checking the new batches. Gage cleaned up and changed into his self-imposed uniform of a Merrick Craft Brewing T-shirt over nice jeans and boots.

The brewery's collection of shirts sold quite well, as did a variety of mugs, pint glasses, and other souvenirs. Merrick Craft Brewing wasn't exactly famous, but it had started to make a name for itself in the Adirondacks, which made Gage very happy.

I've never felt as much at home as I do here. I love living and working here. Now I need a mate, Gage thought.

We're not as young as we used to be. We need to get a move on finding the right person, his Malinois replied.

I'm not going to settle just to have company, Gage cautioned. *I want to find a true mate.*

Don't be too picky. I have needs.

Gage didn't appreciate his Malinois's nagging, but he also didn't disagree. *Go to sleep. I have work to do.*

In response, his Malinois snorted loudly but retreated into a corner of Gage's mind, where he tossed out occasional snarky comments and stayed out of the way.

"Hey, Bobby! How's the new batch going?" Gage asked.

"It's coming along." Bobby was an otter shifter and a Fox Hollow native. Now in his middle years, he had worked for breweries elsewhere in the Adirondacks before coming home to Fox Hollow. "I think this one might be a bit more potent. I tried a different formulation. You'll have to see if your friends notice."

"Did it affect you?"

Bobby laughed. "I stuck around after my shift ended last night and tried it out. Got a nice buzz—but I'm a lightweight compared to the big boys."

Gage had never figured out how the magic of shifting worked when the human form didn't match the bulk of the shifted form. But he knew from the focus groups that shifters who turned into bigger animals—like Brandon's moose—had an even harder time feeling the effects than the smaller creatures, like otters, beavers, and squirrels.

It only took half as much for Liam to get buzzed compared to Russ or Drew. And so far, nothing had affected Brandon—even a little.

Then again, I've seen videos of deer eating fermented apples. Maybe it's a good thing that Brandon isn't a cheap drunk.

"What's it taste like?" Gage accepted a tasting cup and concentrated as he let the flavors bloom on his tongue.

"You tell me, boss." Bobby grinned, clearly proud of his concoction.

"Good body, but not too hoppy." Gage swirled the beer in his mouth. "I'm picking up some jammy undertones—raspberry and fig?"

"Very good. You nailed it. There are always people who prefer a sweeter drink, and this is a little fruitier without taking away from the other elements," Bobby told him. "I think we might be able to win over some skeptics with it."

"I'm all for it," Gage told him. "I love the idea of having something for everyone who chooses to drink. And for the others, there's soda."

Gage had a contract with an Adirondack-based soda maker that produced original flavors unique to the region. The extensive variety was a hit with locals and tourists and set the brewery apart from competitors.

"I've got the gang coming in to try the other new batch. Do you think you'd have enough to try this one on them, too?"

"Sure," Bobby agreed. "Your friends are very willing to tie one on for the team."

"It's a heavy burden, but somehow, they manage," Gage replied melodramatically and laughed. "I really like what you're doing. I think they're both great additions to the menu."

Once he assured himself that all was right with the vats, he headed back to the taproom to check in with the kitchen and wait staff.

"Don't forget, it's RPG Night," he told Shelly, who oversaw the servers.

"Got it, boss. We'll keep checking every half hour for drink refills and snack orders, but everyone knows to make sure the players aren't in the middle of something dramatic," Shelly replied. "We all love listening to the adventures on game night. Some of the players missed their calling in the theater."

Imaginations ran wild on game night, and the players really got into the scenes. Since most were regulars and knew each other well, there was plenty of banter, and everyone stayed friendly.

He checked at the bar. Carlos, the head bartender, was already set for the night's crowd, and he had an extra barback on duty to help keep up with the orders.

"You got the new brews Bobby wants to demo?" Gage asked.

Carlos nodded. "They're in pitchers. We'll keep an eye on the reactions so you have a different perspective from what the drinkers report." He snickered. "Some people have a hard time realizing they're not as sober as they think they are."

"Make sure you let Bobby know your impressions," Gage said. "I really like the flavors."

His last stop was in the kitchen. Cathy, like several of the other section heads, had stayed when Gage bought the brewery. She'd been with the prior owner for ten years and had a good read on the difference in food preferences between nights when the crowd was mostly local versus the tourists.

"Got everything you need?" Gage poked his head in far enough to see that Cathy and her staff already had a good start prepping for the evening.

"I was worried when my grocery order was late, but it got here in time and wasn't missing anything, so we won't be stuck with peanuts and pretzels," Cathy told him with a grin.

Gage knew the regulars would make the best of it if a delivery mishap meant missing out on their favorite snacks, but the evening's receipts would be much higher if they could cater to the gamers' munchies.

Sitting around moving little rocks on a board is not playing, his Malinois objected. *Chasing a ball is playing. Or fetching a stick. I need to teach you about real play.*

Bite me, Gage replied. Since Malinois were sometimes jokingly called Maligators for their hard bite in police settings, the response was an in-joke with his other side.

Humans throw balls around.

We do that sometimes, Gage reminded him.

We could go now. Now is good, his Mal said hopefully.

Not now, sorry. Gotta work to afford your pricy dog treats.

His dog gave a huff and shot him the side-eye, then slunk to a corner of his mind.

Gage spent the rest of the morning in his office paying bills, ordering supplies, and handling paperwork. While those weren't the most exciting parts of owning the brewery, he accepted them as a necessary evil. Fortunately, his coursework and the time he spent working at other breweries prepared him well.

He really enjoyed spending time with Bobby and his other brewers dreaming up new flavors or giving feedback to tweak or perfect a new offering. It surprised Gage how happy he was circulating in the tasting room in the evenings, chatting with friends, neighbors, and tourists about the different flavor profiles.

Gage also liked dreaming up ways to spread the word about the brewery. He had liked his marketing classes in college and loved coming up with promotions, ordering branded tchotchkes, and creating special events that brought people together.

This certainly wasn't the life his family had in mind for him. The Merricks had a long, proud tradition in law enforcement and the military. Gage knew his father and brothers cared about him, but they weren't big on showing affection unless someone was dying, and hid their feelings with macho joking. His father had tried to be accepting; his grandfather much less so. As the youngest, his brothers cut Gage some slack, but being gay tested their tolerance.

Gage finally decided, when he was old enough to choose, that he wasn't cut out for uniforms. He left home for college and visited on holidays now, since he loved his family but realized they worked best together in small doses.

We have a new pack that likes us just fine, his Mal pointed out. Gage loved the way he fit in with his friends in Fox Hollow. His family could be a bit snooty about Malinois being the epitome of a military dog as if that made Mal shifters superior. Here in Fox Hollow, most people didn't have their traditional pack or other family unit to fall back on, so they forged their own regardless of their animal.

We have a great pack—and other awesome friends. I like it here. The cabin is perfect. The brewery is everything I hoped it would be.

But it's not complete without a mate, his Mal finished.

That sounds like a romance drama…but yeah. I'm ready to find the right guy, Gage admitted.

That realization wasn't new. He had always hoped to fall in love and find a partner. But first there was college and then buying the brewery, and Gage had been so consumed by everything involved that looking for love hadn't been the priority.

We'd sleep better with a mate, his Mal argued.

It's got to be the right one. And so far, we haven't met him.

Look harder. It would be good not to be alone, his Mal replied.

We aren't exactly lonely, Gage pointed out. *We have our friends. And the brewery.*

Not the same.

Gage sighed. *I agree. But getting the brewery up and running took everything I had. It wouldn't have been fair to start with someone when I wasn't really present. Now, I can take time away to make it work.*

Don't fart around. I'm tired of waiting.

Sometimes his inner dog reminded him of his gruff, ex-military grandfather, and Gage struggled not to let it raise his hackles—figuratively or literally. *I'm fond of eating on a regular schedule and having a place to live. We had to build the brewery to make that happen. And we're much more attractive to a mate if we aren't starving and living under a bush,* he pointed out.

Just don't take forever. It would be nice to curl up with someone at night, his Mal admitted, relenting on his gruff posture.

You're a big softie, Gage teased. Belgian Malinois could be intimidating, and they were good in their guard dog roles, but they also were deeply connected to family. Striking out on his own when his father didn't support his goals had hurt Gage badly. That went double when his brothers sided with their dad. He wasn't completely estranged—his mother called occasionally with updates, and he got the occasional gift card—but he only went home on holidays, and the time always felt tense.

He had never intended to cut ties. That had been his father's reaction to not being able to order Gage to follow the family path. But Gage had always known he would be miserable as a soldier or in law enforcement, despite how sexy and exciting television and movies made it seem. He realized that learning to brew beer for shifters wasn't as heroic as being security personnel.

And despite changes, he knew being gay would only make fitting in more difficult.

But isn't being able to sit at a bar with friends and have a good time the kind of thing they're fighting to protect? I'm giving people a place to go that isn't work or home, a friendly spot to fit in, a way to meet new people and to not be alone. That might not be heroic, but it's necessary. And maybe I'll meet my person along the way.

CHAPTER 4
GAGE

Gage jotted down new ideas for special events that had occurred to him on his morning run. RPG Night was a big winner, and he thought the library book club would be popular during the winter months. Board games on another evening might attract a different group of people, and themed party nights for holidays with seasonal flavors, special appetizers, and decorations had also been well-received and could be expanded.

He had worked out a deal with several local musicians to rotate through the weekends and wanted to test out occasional craft nights for people who liked to knit or do puzzles. Ask A Brewer Q&As could also draw people, he thought.

We aren't a regular bar, but people need more than tastings to come out and hang around. The nice thing is we can try out new ideas, and if they don't work, come up with something else.

The tasting room wasn't a full restaurant, but it did offer a variety of small plates to nosh on in between trying different brews. Most people stood at the bar, especially if they wanted to try more than one type of beer.

A few high tops were scattered through the room for those who wanted to step back and savor their food and drink without feeling like they were interfering with tastings. A comfortable couch and two armchairs with a coffee table sat against one wall.

Since this was RPG Night, three tables were set up in a U-shape at the opposite end of the room from the bar. Gage felt a little wistful. He played a lot of RPGs, both live and online, when he was in school but his responsibilities with the brewery interfered with being as active as he would like. Now and again, he dropped in on a game, and it always made him nostalgic. *Maybe when things slow down, I can have a night to kick back and play on a regular basis.*

Gage suspected that the brewery crowd might be a little more mellow than the usual barflies who wanted to watch sports. The bar at the Fox Hollow Hotel carried his brews, and Gage didn't see them as competition because the vibe was completely different. The hotel went heavier on live entertainment, trivia nights, and karaoke, and offered full meals. A couple more traditional bars outside town catered to the die-hard sports fans.

Something for everybody—but shifters still can't get a buzz. I want to change that—one brew at a time.

Trying to create a beer that reacted with the unusual metabolisms of paranormal creatures wasn't simple. First of all, the world at large didn't recognize the existence of shifters, vampires, and the like—and keeping it that way was better for everyone. So Gage couldn't rely on completed research for what worked on supernatural body chemistry. If those studies existed, they were locked in a military database somewhere, and Gage definitely didn't want to attract the wrong kind of attention.

Gage went looking for referrals to shifters with a background in chemistry and found a few who were willing to help him figure out whether it was the fermentation process itself that didn't mesh with paranormal physiology, or if key natural additives might create more of an effect. He made sure to purchase through known suppliers since he had heard about ingredients of dubious quality being smuggled in from Canada.

Much trial and error later, the brewery launched its first

enhanced offering, part of its Moon Phases line of specialty beers. Word of mouth let shifters, vampires, werewolves, and others with magical abilities know and attracted both the curious and those desperate to get a buzz.ox Hollow got plenty of seasonal visitors who were mundane humans, and they liked the beer, too—although they had no difficulty feeling the effect. The year-round residents had some sort of psychic or paranormal abilities, a requirement helped along by a bit of magic and real estate agents who were witches.

The alarm on Gage's watch went off, and he wrapped up the office work and closed his laptop. He made the same trek in reverse, popping in to assure himself that the kitchen was humming along, then glanced at the bar and got a nod from Carlos, and finally ended up in the taproom with Bobby.

"All good?" Gage looked around at the people who were starting to trickle in.

"I think we've got it covered, boss," Bobby said. "If this keeps up, we'll have a good crowd tonight."

"Cross your fingers," Gage replied.

He flitted between the rooms, greeting visitors and striking up conversations. Gage lingered in the taproom, eager to see the reactions to the newest formulas. His market research funds were limited, so using his eyes and ears was the best alternative.

The night's gamers had already begun to file in and choose their seats, along with the game-runner, who was setting up his area.

"Hi, Dave," Gage greeted the game-runner and waved at the others. "Ready for tonight's campaign?"

Dave was a programmer for the Fox Institute and never missed game night. He had a loyal group of players but welcomed newcomers. "Always ready. I think I've got some surprises cooked up for the group tonight."

Gage grinned. "I like the sound of that. Just keep the sound effects to a dull roar. We don't want to alarm the visitors."

Dave nodded. "Don't freak the mundanes. Got it."

Gage wandered away, observing more than playing host. The locals knew he owned the place, but visitors were more likely to speak candidly if they weren't aware of his connection.

"Have you been here before? How good is the brew?"

Gage turned to meet the gaze of a very handsome blond with green eyes. It took him a moment to find his voice. He felt a zing of energy he had never sensed before and took a half-step closer instinctively, part attraction, part protectiveness.

Mate, his Mal said. *Don't you feel it? He's ours.*

"I've been here plenty of times. I think the brew's pretty awesome." Gage managed to string words together and stop staring.

"Good to know. Are you a beer fiend? I'm still learning my way around things that aren't sold at the grocery store," the stranger replied.

Gage smiled. "Yeah, I'm a fan—and I like to try new flavors and types. So much more interesting than the same-old, same-old."

Be clever. Impress him. Don't let him get away, his Mal urged.

"I'm Gage." He hoped he didn't look distracted listening to a voice only he could hear.

"Scott," the blond replied. "Do you live in Fox Hollow?"

"I do now," Gage replied. "Moved here from Schenectady." He paused. "I don't think I've seen you around."

When Gage shook hands, he felt a stronger zing that seemed to confirm his Mal's insistence that Scott was someone special.

"I came up to the mountains to get out of Albany for a change. It's beautiful up here."

Convince him to move here. We need our mate, Gage's other half prodded.

"Fox Hollow is a great place." Gage was disappointed that Scott might only be passing through. "The year-round population isn't big, but we get plenty of visitors spring through fall. Winter takes a special breed."

"I bet. Albany gets lots of snow, and it's a couple of hours south of here," Scott said.

Gage didn't get the sense that Scott was a shifter. He was usually pretty good at sensing other shape-changers. He wasn't a vampire, and he didn't have the unsettled energy that Gage associated with were creatures. But he picked up *something*—he just wasn't sure what.

"While you're in town, stop by the Fox Institute. They've got a really interesting small museum on psychic phenomena." Gage watched for a reaction. A slight twitch suggested that Scott recognized the name.

"I've heard of it. Do you believe in that sort of thing?" Scott asked.

Gage had the feeling they were dancing around each other, but he wasn't entirely sure why. He definitely felt a strong physical attraction, which went with meeting one's mate—if that's what Scott was. *It's been a long dry spell. He's cute, and I could just be horny.*

He chose his words carefully, not wanting to scare Scott away. Although if he was resistant to the idea of the supernatural being real their pairing was doomed from the start.

"I think there are a lot of things that don't fit the usual explanations," Gage answered. "I like to keep an open mind."

"Tactful—but not exactly what I asked." Scott tossed the conversational ball back into Gage's court with a smile.

Might as well go balls to the wall right up front. This isn't going to work if he's a committed non-believer. Gage's intuition told him Scott was trying to feel him out on the subject. *I'd rather he felt me up, but that's for another time.* He wondered why but didn't sense a threat.

"I know people over at the Institute, and I believe that their gifts are real. They have different psychic abilities, which I don't pretend to understand and can't explain. But from everything I've seen and heard, I think they are what they claim to be." Gage hoped he didn't sound defensive.

Please don't let him be some type of myth buster who came here to look for fakes. He's far too cute—I'll be very disappointed.

Scott nodded. "I know someone there too. Thought I'd stop by and pay my regards while I'm in town. For what it's worth, I think there's something to the whole psychic thing. I can't explain it, but I've known people who have the Sight, and I believe it's real."

Gage felt a wave of relief. *That's one hurdle down. But it's a big stretch from believing someone can read Tarot cards to accepting shifters.*

"They're always adding new programs at the Institute," Gage said, eager to keep the conversation going. "Who do you know over there? We might have some friends in common."

"I knew Dr. Jeffries. He was one of my professors at Ithaca," Scott replied. "I haven't seen him in years, but I really enjoyed his classes. I don't know if he'll remember me."

"Of course he will." Gage tapped his temple with two fingers. "Psychic—remember?"

Scott laughed. "I guess you're right. I didn't realize he had left Ithaca, but when I looked him up online, he seems to have gotten a promotion with his job at the Institute. I'm happy for him."

"Anyone else?"

"I read a book called *Everyday Psychics* by one of the professors there. I think it's fascinating how the author recognizes small powers. He believes people can use them to do important things, even though they aren't the sort of abilities most folks think about when someone talks about psychics," Scott replied.

"I liked that book." Gage felt his heartbeat speed up as he found common ground. "I read it right after I moved here. I wanted to understand the Institute better and the people who attend. I learned a lot."

Scott looked around. "Is there a private party? I can come back another night."

Gage shook his head. "No—the taproom has themed events.

Tonight is RPG Night. We have a core of regulars, but new people are always welcome."

"We?" Scott asked.

Before Gage could answer, Bobby slipped up beside him. "Hey, boss. Sorry to interrupt, but someone has a question about allergens."

"Boss? This is your brewery?"

"Busted." Gage gave Scott an apologetic look. "Sorry. Gotta go. Try one of the brews—I'd love to hear what you think. I'll find you later."

Gage let Bobby lead him away, struggling not to cast a backward glance in Scott's direction.

"Bad timing?" Bobby asked. "Sorry about that. You can always buy him a flight when you're done."

The allergy issue took only minutes to handle, but Gage knew he had earned a grateful patron who could relax and enjoy the drinks without worrying. Afterward, he caught Carlos's eye at the bar, and ordered a flight delivered to where Scott sat at the end of the bar.

"Sure thing, boss." Carlos's raised eyebrow spoke volumes. Gage usually circulated through the taproom, but he didn't make a habit of flirting. Most of the time, he was too busy making sure everything went smoothly.

Gage realized now that he had been so deeply focused on the brewery's business that he had ignored everything else. Now that the taproom was up and running in the black, he knew— even without his Mal's nudging—that it was time to think about more than work.

He watched from the other end of the bar as Carlos delivered the flight and told Scott that Gage had sent it. Scott smiled and nodded his thanks, accepting the gift. That gave Gage the courage to approach him.

My people skills are rusty. I'm way out of practice.

It would be good to claim our mate while your dick still works, his Mal pointed out. *Although I guess you could go to the vet for pills.*

You go to the vet. I go to a doctor, Gage corrected.

A vet is a doctor. I like our vet. He gives me treats, and the cute vet tech scratches my ears. Does anyone at your doctor's office scratch your ears?

Gage privately thought that his general practitioner was a hottie, but there was absolutely no chemistry between them. The lack of attraction was helpful when all that covered his reaction was a thin paper sheet. *You know they don't.*

Hmph. Clearly my doctor is better, his inner dog gloated.

Gage made his way through the crowd to edge in beside Scott. "Did you try them? Have you found a favorite?"

"I was hoping you'd come over, and we could do it together," Scott replied. The ambiguous wording went right to Gage's groin even though he doubted that was Scott's intention.

Standing close to Scott, Gage could pick up his scent—a woodsy-lemon undertone that raised a slew of emotions as well as Gage's dick. *Home. Companion. Lover. Mate.*

Someone bumped into Scott, and Gage felt a surge of protectiveness. *Mine.*

Gage hoped his strained smile covered the war between his shifter side and human politeness.

"I'd love to get your reactions." Gage kept eye contact with Scott. "Want to get a table? It's crowded here."

"Sure. Lead the way, *boss,*" Scott replied with a wink that Gage felt in his stomach. Scott carried the board with the flight glasses, and on their way, Gage flagged a server and ordered a soft pretzel.

Go slow. He's cute but we don't know him, his Mal cautioned.

He's not going to roofie me in my own bar. And you were just pushing to speed things up.

True. Still, strangers are dangerous, his guard dog replied.

My plan is to strip search him and check body crevices. But we've got rituals before we can sniff butts, Gage replied.

No need to be condescending.

"Gage?" Scott's prompt told Gage he'd been in his head for too long.

"Sorry—just thought of something I need to do later," Gage replied. "Now, I'm really interested to see what you think about the brews."

"How potent are they? I have to drive back to my motel."

"I'll get you a rideshare if you need it," Gage promised. *He's in a motel. Just passing through? That would be a pity. He's awfully fine. Need to give him a reason to stay.*

"Is this really your taproom?"

Gage couldn't help grinning. "Yeah. My pride and joy—and the reason I don't get out much. I bought it from the previous owner, and we've been experimenting with new recipes since then."

Gage tried to pick up vibes to indicate whether Scott had any supernatural abilities. He sensed a faint buzz of energy he usually associated with psychics, but it felt muted. *Maybe some native talent but undeveloped? Interesting.*

Close proximity just reinforced Gage's certainty that Scott was his mate. Interestingly, he didn't get any sense that his crush was also a shifter.

We can work with that. There are plenty of mixed marriages in town, his Mal encouraged.

That's not what that term means.

It could if you wanted it to, his dog countered.

Gage ignored that last comment and focused on Scott. His pretty green eyes reminded Gage of the water in the Caribbean.

I've barely met the man, and I'm already sappy. Maybe love at first sight really does exist.

"So this one," Gage turned his attention to the first glass on the board, "is Wulfbayne. Try it, and tell me what you think." He made sure their fingers brushed as he took one of the glasses from the board and handed it to Scott.

To his credit, Scott seemed to know how to do a testing. He sniffed the liquid, then took a sip and swirled it in his mouth before swallowing. "Interesting. Dark, but with notes of raspberry and chocolate."

Gage pushed another beer toward Scott. "This is Immortal Kiss. I'm curious about what you taste."

Scott thought before replying. "That could be seriously addictive. It's a little lighter with some blood orange and caramel tones."

"You've got a knack for this." Gage was mesmerized by Scott's lips and the flick of his tongue between sips.

"You're a very good teacher," Scott replied, and Gage didn't miss the undertone. "I'm usually a quick study."

He smells interested, Gage's Mal informed him. *Go for it.*

That gave Gage all kinds of naughty thoughts, but it was still far too soon. "The third one is Shyftt."

Scott seemed to be enjoying their proximity as much as he was the beer. Gage sat close but intentionally didn't bump together or box Scott in with his knees. Three beers in, and Scott had moved forward several inches so his knee brushed Gage's inner thigh.

He likes us, his Mal supplied as if Gage was a clueless virgin.

"It's good," Scott replied. "Orange undertones, and is that butterscotch?"

"Yep." Gage thought how much he would like to lick the sticky topping off Scott's naked body. "That's a hard combination for most people to pick out. You've got a talented tongue." He was blatantly flirting and held his breath to see how Scott would react.

"So I've been told." Scott gave a side glance that showed off long lashes.

Gage adjusted himself in his seat and cleared his throat. He felt his cheeks heat and saw a glint of mischief in Scott's gaze that told him the other knew exactly what he was doing.

"Number four is WitchyWooWoo." Gage left his knee pressed against Scott's leg.

Despite the distraction, Scott was paying attention to the tasting, giving thoughtful answers. Gage appreciated the input but wondered if he needed to up his game if Scott's whole brain hadn't gone south yet.

"That's a little brisk," Scott replied. "Apple. A hint of basil. And I'm getting a whiff of juniper."

Gage nodded. "I'm impressed. Last one—Magick Dreams. What do you think?"

Scott swirled the liquid in his mouth and thought for a moment. "Jammy, with an undertone of coffee. Fig? And maybe a little bit of rhubarb."

"You're a natural." Gage was sincerely impressed with Scott's ability to identify what he tasted and put it into words. "Most people know when they like something, but they can't pick out the notes. Great job!"

"They're all good," Scott said. "And they're original brews?"

Gage nodded, blushing a bit with how proud he was of the brewery. "All unique to our brewery. We've got a great brewmaster, and he likes to keep everyone on their toes."

What Gage left out, for now, was that each of the brews was specially formulated to work with the unique metabolisms of shifters, weres, vampires, and witches so that they could get at least a buzz before burning off the alcohol completely.

That's on a need-to-know basis, and he doesn't need to know yet. Gage sincerely hoped that even though Scott didn't seem to have a paranormal side, he could still come to accept and appreciate the supernatural.

"Did you always know you wanted to brew beer?" Scott worked his way through the rest of the glasses, finishing them off in reverse order. Gage nudged the soft pretzel and a glass of water toward him. Scott pulled off a piece, dunked it in mustard, and wrapped his lips around it for a second before taking a bite.

He's a tease. This is going to be fun.

"For a long time." Gage struggled to raise his gaze to Scott's eyes instead of his mesmerizing lips. "I got a degree in applied science and worked in taprooms and breweries ever since I was old enough to serve. I love the creativity of making a totally new drink for people to enjoy."

"You seem to be doing well." Scott glanced around the busy room.

Gage shrugged and felt his cheeks color. "We're in the black —which is better than a lot of breweries. Summer is crazy with all the tourists, but we're lucky to have a supportive community. Fox Hollow is a special place."

"It seems nice," Scott said.

"Are you here for business or pleasure?" Gage asked, not trying to keep the insinuation from his tone.

"Maybe both?" Scott answered with mischief in his eyes.

"Sounds like a plan." Gage brushed his knee against Scott's leg.

"Do you ever leave the brewery? Maybe we could have dinner and talk when it's a little quieter?" Scott's grin faltered just a bit, leaving him looking a little uncertain.

"That sounds good," Gage replied.

Just then, Bobby waved to him, indicating that he needed Gage. "Oops. Duty calls. Sorry. The flight and pretzel are on the house. That's a blatant ploy to encourage you to come back."

"I'm buying dinner," Scott said. "That's a blatant ploy to get you to come." A hint of a smile made it clear his wording was intentional.

Oh, it's on, Gage thought.

"What are you doing tomorrow night?" Scott asked. "Even busy brewery owners need to eat dinner."

Gage pretended to think for a moment, not wanting to look too easy, although he already knew his calendar was clear. "I'm open. What time?"

"Is it better to go early so we have time to talk, and you can get back here for happy hour?"

Gage appreciated the thoughtfulness of the question but shook his head. "Bobby can handle opening. The staff will probably appreciate having me out of their hair for a while."

"How's the food at the Fox Hollow Hotel? It's the only place I know in town," Scott admitted.

"The food is good, and so's the service, and they won't mind us lingering at the table this time of year," Gage said. They agreed on a time, and Scott made sure to brush his fingers against Gage's hand.

So you're going to sleep with him? His Mal sounded hopeful and horny.

Slow your roll. If he's really our mate, it'll work out. We're flirting. There's a process.

Ah. Circling and sniffing. I understand," his Malinois replied.

Not exactly, but now isn't the time to explain. Watch and learn.

Gage went to deal with an issue over someone's bill. He expected Scott to be gone by the time he came back to the main room and was pleasantly surprised to find him nursing a glass of water and a cup of coffee, watching the gamers as they joked and played their roles.

He took Scott's procrastination as a good sign. It meant he would be okay to drive back to his motel, but it also likely indicated that he felt comfortable at the taproom and liked the vibe.

Of course he does. We are here—his mate. On some level, he knows, his Mal asserted confidently.

You think so? Gage had never been smooth when it came to dating. In his younger days, when his focus was on school, he had missed prime opportunities because he had been oblivious. Later, he hadn't paid attention at all; not wanting the distraction while building the taproom took his full concentration.

It's good you're so pretty, because you can be slow, his Malinois replied in a long-suffering tone.

Hey. I'm you. So if I'm slow, so are you.

I'm also very pretty, his shifter asserted.

You didn't answer. Do you think Scott wants more than a one-night stand? I don't even know if he's planning to stay in Fox Hollow. He never did answer my question about why he's here. Gage hadn't realized until he walked away that Scott didn't offer a reply.

It's probably something boring and he didn't think you'd be interested.

Maybe he's undercover with the ABC. The state's beverage control sometimes sent agents to make sure bars were complying with the law, not serving minors, and avoiding overserving. *He could be a spy. I didn't even get his last name.*

We are going to have dinner with him. You can find out more then. All that matters is that he liked and desired us. The nose knows, his Mal said with a confidence Gage didn't entirely feel.

If he isn't a shifter, we'll have to have the talk. There's no telling how that will go, Gage warned his other half.

He's our mate. It will be all right. And he has something special to him too.

You felt that? Gage asked.

Magic of some sort. We are magic too. See—it's fate.

You're a hopeless romantic, Gage accused affectionately. He was extremely fond of his Malinois and knew that under the rough-tough first impression, he was really a big softie.

We need to stop sleeping alone. That's practical, not just romantic.

Sure thing, tough guy. Your secret is safe with me, Gage teased.

GAGE ATE breakfast and drove to a new section of Fox Hollow Park, where a flatbed truck held new trees in root balls to plant before the weather turned cold.

"Glad you made it, Gage," his friend Matt hailed him. "I just finished marking where the trees will go. You're doing me a big solid, helping out like this."

"Happy to help—and you're giving me a chance to dig without getting in trouble. How deep do you want me to go?"

Gage stepped behind the open door to his truck to shed his clothes and make the change, nudging the door shut with his nose as his Malinois.

"Stop before you get to China." Matt laughed. "For real? About as deep as your shoulders."

Gage gave an abrupt nod to show he understood, followed by a sharp bark.

"Go get 'em," Matt encouraged.

Gage bounded off, giving in to the sensory overload of smells and textures. He chased a bug, sniffed a particularly interesting plant, and ran zoomies around the cleared area several times before getting down to business.

He set off at a run, heading for the first marked area like it was a timed competition. In each spot where Matt wanted a hole, four stakes marked the sides. Gage picked one spot and started digging, sending the dirt flying, lost in the sheer joy of movement.

The ground was still moist from a recent rain. Gage's big paws and strong muscles made it easy, and he loved the feel and smell of wet earth. When he was digging, Gage let his human worries fade to the back of his mind. In the excitement of excavating, he unearthed rocks and worms and tossed them into the air as he cleared more space.

It didn't take long until he had opened a hole wide enough for him to sit in and up to his dog shoulders. He gave a sharp bark, leaped out, and headed for the next marked area.

"Great job, Gage!" Matt called out. He supervised from several feet away where he leaned on a small backhoe to smooth out the sides of the holes and get them ready for planting.

By the time Gage finished the spots for the other trees, he was covered in mud. He shook off, sending larger clods flying, then padded up to Matt with a big grin of satisfaction.

"Wow. That was awesome. And the ground around the holes isn't torn up from the backhoe tread. Thank you."

Gage barked twice in enthusiastic agreement, then turned in circles, hoping Matt got his message.

"You want me to hose you off? Come over to the side of the

bathroom building where the hose is," Matt told him. "I'm going to get your clothes for afterward."

Gage padded over to wait by the hose. Matt set his clothes where they wouldn't get wet.

"As soon as you're not a muddy mess, I'll take the stack into the bathroom and you can change in one of the stalls. There's a towel too," Matt assured him.

Gage barked his thanks. Matt turned the hose on him, and Gage leaped and spun, playing in the stream as much as he bathed. Matt laughed, making it a game to catch Gage with the water as Gage dodged and bounded. Since he was a full-grown Malinois, he could jump to be at eye level with his friend.

Finally, he settled and let Matt thoroughly spray him off, removing the last of the mud. Matt stood back as Gage shook off again, sending water everywhere.

"Go change. You're a menace," Matt joked.

Gage intentionally shook a little near his friend in response. Matt grumbled, but there was no heat behind his words.

The hose had taken off the worst of the dirt, but Gage intended to shower once he got home—especially if there was a chance he and Scott might take things further between them than the last time.

He daydreamed as he dressed, thinking about the chemistry he sensed between them at the taproom and the certainty of his Mal that they were mates.

Of course I'm certain. I'm your better half, his Mal asserted with confidence.

Don't start that again, Gage protested, but affection colored his tone. This was an old sparring match with his shifter side.

I'm faster, I can bite harder, and I jump higher, his Malinois challenged.

I can drive a car, read a book, and get money out of an ATM to buy food, Gage pointed out.

Valid. But I can run faster, know what's going on in the forest from the scents, and hunt dinner if I had to.

We still don't know if Scott has anything supernatural about him besides maybe some psychic stuff. He might not react well when he finds out you and I are a package deal, Gage warned.

How could anyone not be impressed by our awesomeness? his Mal responded, but Gage heard a note of hurt.

Hey, don't get mopy.

I don't mope.

You totally do, Gage countered. *Remember the time we were going to get ice cream, and the truck was gone when we went for cones? You moped all evening.*

That was different. I'd been looking forward to that all day, his Mal sulked. *And a mate is not ice cream. He wouldn't smell like mate if he weren't.*

Gage understood his dog's worry. Being a shifter didn't come with a user manual, and while Fox Hollow was much better than most places for supernatural creatures, there weren't how-to classes he had ever heard of. He had picked up the essentials from his parents and watched his older brothers figure out their other half, but no one had covered things like falling in love with a non-shifter or how to explain to a mundane.

As far as I can tell, he's very interested in us that way. Definitely boyfriend material. And tonight maybe we'll take things further and figure out more about us.

What's to figure out? Mate.

Gage knew his Mal was being intentionally stubborn, but he let him have his moment. It was how his other half sorted out feelings and figured his way through problems, and Gage was used to the grumpiness.

Don't you remember the TV shows? Even humans take time to catch on about falling in love.

I always figured that was exaggerated to make shifters feel better, his dog grumped.

Newsflash, clueless—those shows are written for humans. That's really how they are. Well, maybe not always quite so dramatic, but more true than not.

Gage had spent his life observing and learning about the non-shifters around him. Part of that came from wanting to blend in, but he had also been curious about the differences and similarities.

Mixed marriages were fairly rare and sometimes frowned upon, but not unknown. Scott knew couples in town that were a mix of human and shifter or psychic and nil. While many people with supernatural abilities tended to marry someone with similar gifts, there was plenty of evidence that wanting the relationship badly enough could overcome the difficulties.

Before he moved to Fox Hollow, Gage had been surrounded by regular people without special gifts. He didn't know how they managed.

When he got home, Gage cleaned up the house in case he could get Scott to come back with him. He took a shower, getting the last grit out from beneath his nails and washing away the rain and sweat. He used his best-smelling shampoo and made sure to manscape, hoping for the best.

He chose a black V-neck shirt that went well with his hair and a pair of jeans that showed off his muscular legs and fine ass. Gage couldn't help turning sideways in the mirror to check himself out.

You look pretty good—although your ears are a little small, his Mal snarked.

Bite me.

Malinois had large, pointy ears that seemed a little too big for their heads. Gage thought his dog side was handsome, but they often joked about the ears.

Gage blew out a deep breath, trying not to be nervous. *I already know we have chemistry. We like each other, and we've flirted. I'm fine if we don't go any farther tonight—there's no rush.*

Or is there? I don't really know anything about what brought him to town. He dodged a real answer. Is he with the government? Law enforcement? Ohh...maybe he's a spy. Spies are sexy. But they aren't really marriage material.

Gage didn't just want a hot couple of nights. He was ready to settle down and find his forever man. So was his Mal—who seemed convinced that Scott was his fated mate.

Does Scott feel that too? If not, is the mate bond real? And if he doesn't pick up on something like that, how could I ever convince him without sounding nuts?

Gage shook his head to clear it, resolving to take things one day at a time.

I can't make this happen faster than it's going to on its own. Pushing won't help. But I sure wish we could skip to the good part where we fall in love and get our happily ever after.

CHAPTER 5
SCOTT

Scott let himself into the motel room after leaving the brewery and leaned against the door, heart still aflutter after flirting with Gage.

What just happened? I get a taste of chocolate and strawberries when I see him. That means romance. And what was up with that little energy zing when we touched? I know I didn't imagine that. It's never happened before. Could Gage be the one?

Gage pressed every one of Scott's buttons when it came to attraction. He was tall, dark-haired, muscular, confident but not obnoxious, and charming without seeming to work at it.

What are the odds that I walk into a bar on my own time that not only has someone who might be my forever guy but also happens to be on my list of people from SPAM to check out?

It wasn't intentional. I didn't even realize that until later. Shit—when he finds out what I do, will he believe me that I'm not playing with his heart to get information?

I probably shouldn't go on our date while I'm here working. Then again, I didn't get a danger vibe. Pretty much the opposite. And if he is specially formulating his brew, that's not illegal as long as he's not sourcing ingredients from smugglers.

Everything about Gage checked off boxes. His deep voice, the confident way he walked, his humor, and the sense of safety he radiated like he would keep Scott protected from danger.

Kind of funny since I'm the secret agent, the guy with the gun. But I feel like nothing bad is going to happen to me as long as Gage is around.

Scott thought about what a roller coaster ride the last few weeks had been—getting laid off, being hired by SPAM, moving to Albany, his whirlwind training and orientation, having his eyes opened to the reality of supernatural creatures, and being sent off on his first assignment—where he might have just met his mate.

I've always thought that the whole one day can change your life thing was just a meme, but I feel like everything's been turned topsy-turvy like shaking a snow globe.

Scott liked what he had seen so far of Fox Hollow enough that he had to remind himself why he came to town.

No one I've met so far seems like a drug kingpin. It makes sense they'd keep it on the down low. But this is a pretty small town. If someone is running dangerous drugs for shifters, it would be hard to keep it a secret.

He started his day by heading for the Fox Institute, wondering if his former professor would remember him. Scott stopped at the front desk and gave his name, then hung back nervously as she called upstairs.

"Scott!" Dr. Jeffries called out to him as he came down the stairs, grinning in welcome. "It's been a while."

"Good to see you too," Scott said as they exchanged an enthusiastic handshake.

"Come up to my office. We have some catching up to do." Dr. Jeffries looked to the receptionist. "Please hold my calls."

She nodded in acknowledgment.

Jeffries ushered Scott into a comfortably appointed office. His former professor looked much the same as the last time Scott had seen him, just a little older.

And I'm not a kid anymore myself.

"Have a seat. How have you been? Last I heard, you were writing food reviews. Have you come to put the Fox Hollow foodie scene on the map?"

Scott appreciated the warm welcome and was pleasantly surprised that Jeffries had kept up a bit with his career. He reminded himself that his former professor was psychic. Scott didn't know how much the other man could pick up from his thoughts about his reason for coming to town.

"I'm always looking for good places to review," Scott said, keeping his cover. He did still intend to write food reviews on his personal blog, something SPAM had encouraged to keep up his cover.

"Well, you've picked the right town," Jeffries said with genuine enthusiasm. "People take good food seriously here. We have the best donuts in New York State, and everything at the hotel bar is top-notch. There's also a craft brewery you won't want to miss."

"That's actually something I wanted to talk to you about," Scott said. "I've heard that people have been smuggling super-charged alcohol and other drugs in from Canada. Have you heard anything about that sort of thing in Fox Hollow?"

Jeffries looked at him closely, looking less open, more wary, and a little sad. "Let's start over," he suggested. "I can help you best if you tell me what you really need."

That was a polite way of catching Scott in a lie, and he tried not to wince.

"I work for a government agency called SPAM that tries to stop supernatural threats," he replied.

"Like the canned meat?" Jeffries raised an eyebrow.

"Unfortunately, yes. Special Processing And Management. There have been problems with illegal pharmaceuticals and recreational drugs that were altered to affect paranormal metabolisms. The substances are being smuggled, there's no oversight or quality control, and people have died. And because it's being done illegally, safeguards and taxes aren't being observed."

"And you're in Fox Hollow looking for illicit drugs and smugglers?" Jeffries looked a little disappointed, which made Scott wince despite his official authorization.

"The town has a reputation for being more open to people with special abilities than most places," Scott replied. "I was hoping that if you had heard anything, you might point me in the right direction."

Jeffries sat back, quiet for a moment as if he tried to decide what to say. "Have you talked with Sheriff Armel?"

Scott shook his head. "I've been trying to go slow, see what kind of read I get from people."

Jeffries looked closely at him. "You had clairgustance if I recall."

"Yes, that's right." He was surprised Jeffries remembered, although the talent was fairly rare and more likely to be the butt of jokes than taken seriously.

"You're aware of Fox Hollow's rather unique history?"

"It's a haven for psychics and other people with paranormal abilities if the rumors are true," Scott replied. "I don't want to mess that up. I've got no intention of bringing the mundane feds in on anything. I just need to stop some bad people and dangerous substances from causing harm."

"What are you hearing?"

Scott hesitated, trying to decide how much to confide in Jeffries. On one hand, his former professor might steer him toward important clues. But if he felt Scott threatened the town, Jeffries was likely to clam up.

He decided that it was better to have an ally and risk having secrets revealed than alienate his old friend and be frozen out. He suspected that the residents could circle the wagons very quickly even if they were not involved in anything illegal if they feared danger to their town.

"We know that coyotes are bringing illegal drugs and pharmaceuticals in from Canada that have been altered to work with heightened supernatural metabolisms," Scott said. "There's no quality control, no oversight. There have been deaths."

"Coyotes? The animals?"

Scott chuckled. "That's a term for drug smugglers, although in this case, they're also coyote shifters."

"What kind of supernatural creatures are you familiar with besides psychics?"

Scott shifted in his chair, uncomfortable like he was taking a pop quiz. "Shifters. Vampires. Were-creatures. Just like with humans, if individuals are inclined to be dangerous, they're doubly so under the influence."

Jeffries didn't blink at the list, confirming what Scott had already been told in his briefing.

"Tell me about the pharmaceuticals."

"We understand the need for medicine that works on special metabolisms," Scott replied. "There's a big gap right now because the human manufacturers don't know about paranormal people, and neither does most of the government. So the FDA isn't involved checking for safety, reliability, and purity with the medicines being created independently for paranormals. That leaves the door open for bad actors—and for people getting hurt."

"What's the alternative? Sick people need medicine that works for them. Taking really high doses of regular drugs can cause bad side effects. Getting the FDA involved means risking having people with special skills hauled away to labs or imprisoned 'for their own protection,'" Jeffries countered. "Mundane druggists have compounded medications for centuries to work with unique conditions. That's not illegal."

"The problem is, we don't know who's making the substances, whether they do what they claim to do, and what kind of quality control is involved," Scott replied.

"And you think that's going on in Fox Hollow?" Jeffries looked concerned.

"No. But it's a community filled with people with paranormal abilities, and it's not far from the Canadian border. It's a logical place to ask questions."

"We have witches and energy healers and potioners who help people when mundane medicine doesn't work," Jeffries pointed out. "Folk cures have been around for centuries. Many of those are effective, and they're not regulated. They often incorporate the same substances that get used in manufactured pharmaceuticals."

Scott raised his hands, palms out, in a gesture of truce. "I agree. I just want to keep dangerous stuff from hurting people." He paused. "That craft brewery—have they adjusted their recipes for local tastes?"

Jeffries raised an eyebrow. "Have you talked with Gage? However he's formulated his recipes, he's not hurting anyone."

"How do we know that without analysis?" Scott definitely didn't want to find out Gage was a bad guy, but he also had a job to do.

"People with supernatural metabolisms have trouble getting a buzz," Jeffries told him. "That's the big problem overall with any kind of medicine—it either takes a lot more to have an effect, or it burns off too fast, or there are reactions or side effects people without abilities don't have."

He met Scott's gaze. "I understand the need for quality assurance. But I also think that people with powers deserve medicines that work for them, and I'm the last person to deny someone a beer buzz on a Friday night."

"I agree."

"And there's a whole industry producing natural remedies for mundanes that isn't regulated," Jeffries pointed out. "They slap a warning notice on the box, and everyone keeps going."

"That might be an option," Scott said, considering. "I'm new with the agency. I could recommend a review for that."

In the short period of time since he came to Fox Hollow, Scott admitted he had succumbed to the town's charm—and fallen for a certain craft brewer. He didn't want to cause harm to either the town or Gage, but he also had a job to do and needed to stop people from getting hurt.

"How about this?" Jeffries said. "I will ask around on your behalf. I'll need to blow your cover so people understand why you're asking, but only to those I know I can trust, and if there's been scuttlebutt, I'll relay it."

Scott was new to the rules for networking, but Jeffries's proposal sounded like a godsend. "Doesn't that put you in a bind?"

Jeffries frowned. "Yes—and no. I don't think any of our regular residents would be involved in something like that, so I'm not worried about narcing on a friend. If there's someone from outside who is making this area their base to bring in illegal substances and distribute them, it's absolutely a matter for law enforcement."

"Thank you. I appreciate the help—and the trust," Scott replied.

Jeffries fixed him with a look. "The trust goes both ways. Part of helping you is me trying to shield the town from unwanted attention or disclosure. Do you understand what I'm saying?"

Scott nodded. "Absolutely. And, thank you."

"Seems like it's to everyone's benefit to get this matter settled. What will you do afterward, now that you know about Fox Hollow?"

Scott felt his face redden. "I like it here. Technically, I can work from anywhere, so if I got clearance from the Albany office, I could relocate here. It's not a bad drive."

"We're not exactly a hub of excitement most of the time," Jeffries warned. "Although the summer season is fun, and there's a big snowmobile race in the winter."

"I get sent out on assignment, so I'm not sure that where I

live matters as much as that I can get to where I need to go relatively quickly."

"We've got an airport in Saranac Lake that goes to most major airports on the East Coast," Jeffries told him. "If you need something bigger, Burlington and Albany aren't far. Fox Hollow is a great place to live—if you don't mind snow and cold weather. I liked Ithaca, but I'd never go back."

What Jeffries described made Scott's heart ache just a little, naming a void he hadn't been able to put into words. *A home. A community. A place where it's not just anonymous strangers. And maybe…a mate.*

"Can I ask a protocol question?" Scott felt a stab of nervousness and realized he was tapping his fingers on his thigh.

"Sure. What's on your mind?"

"How do you ask someone what their special talent is without being rude?" He felt sure that his blush gave him away.

"Those sorts of things are open secrets—once people get to know and trust you," Jeffries replied. "Sometimes it comes up out of necessity if there's an emergency. But usually, we tell people who we are as part of getting to know them, just like whether or not we hate anchovies or love football."

"It's a bit bigger than anchovies." Scott laughed.

"I guess I've gotten used to things here because it doesn't seem monumental in Fox Hollow. Outside, where we have to hide to be safe—definitely." Jeffries paused. "If you can find the smugglers, you're doing all the communities around here a favor because that sort of thing always ends up causing violence. It would just go over better here if you go through the right channels."

"I'll talk to the sheriff," Scott promised.

"And don't let Gage find out through the grapevine. I think you two might hit it off—but he's very protective and stubborn. When you know him better, you'll understand."

Scott suspected there was more to that statement than it

seemed, but he trusted Jeffries's advice and his psychic insight. "Will do. Thank you for your time—and for trusting me."

His next stop was the sheriff's office. Sheriff Armel was a big, burly man with dark hair and a five-o'clock shadow. Now that he knew Fox Hollow's secret, Scott started playing a mental game of shifter or psychic, and if he picked shifter, guessing what kind.

Armel was definitely a bear.

"Dr. Jeffries let me know you'd be coming." Armel ushered Scott into his office and closed the door. "How can I be of help."

Scott flashed his badge. Armel actually paid attention. "SPAM? Can't say I've heard of you—well, the agency, not the ham."

Scott sighed. "We get that a lot. I believe petitions have been filed to find a new name, but I'm a little afraid of what they might pick next."

To his surprise, Armel gave a hearty laugh. "You could be right on that—quit while you're ahead. Now, how come a fed is in Fox Hollow?"

Scott laid out the whole story once more, explaining about the smuggling and the illicit drugs, as well as the issue around unregulated formulation. Armel listened intently, fingers tented in front of him, brown eyes narrowed in thought.

"Why here?" the sheriff finally said. "There are plenty of towns between Fox Hollow and the border and in the Adirondack Park closer to the line."

"I had to start somewhere, and I heard rumors that Fox Hollow was friendly to people with extra abilities," Scott replied.

"I'd appreciate any help you can provide in squelching those rumors," Armel rumbled. "We don't need that kind of attention."

"Of course. I'm not here to cause trouble. I'd like to help you avoid problems."

Armel snorted. "Typical fed. We're from the government, and we're here to help."

Scott winced. The stereotype was well-earned, and he didn't question Armel's skepticism, but he still thought of himself as one of the good guys, and from what he knew, SPAM didn't seem like an agency of evil.

"I don't want people to get hurt." Scott tried to be as plain-spoken as possible. Armel seemed like a good guy, and since his cover was already blown, he figured he might as well put his cards on the table.

"I get that people with a paranormal metabolism need medications that aren't being supplied through the normal channels," Scott continued. "But that also means that the people who take those pharmaceuticals aren't protected by the normal studies and clinical trials. At least those have doctors watching their patients for bad effects. The recreational drugs—even the mild ones—don't have anyone keeping track. We find out about a bad batch when folks turn up dead."

"I've heard about problems elsewhere," Armel admitted. "We haven't had issues here. I'm not Pollyanna enough to think that things *couldn't* go wrong in Fox Hollow, but honestly, it's harder to get away with things with so many psychics around."

"True. And I'm glad for you. Other towns are getting hit, and some of the drugs are making their way to bigger cities. The problem is spreading. And all our intel points to coyotes coming across the border and into the Adirondacks as the main path," Scott said. "If you have a better idea of how to find the people responsible, I'm all ears."

"Coyotes who are actual coyotes, huh," Armel chuckled. "That's as good as SEALS that are seal shifters. And, I guess, being a bear who is also a Smokey."

Scott relaxed a little. "Thank you for understanding. I wanted a chance to get a sense of the place before I started flashing my badge around."

"The thing is, while the Adirondacks are wild, it's rather misleading," Armel said. "Go due north and cross the border, and you're not far from Montreal. Go northwest, and there's

Ottawa. So while you have the big city drug maker possibility, there's more wilderness on our side than on theirs for them to hide."

"These guys don't need a big operation to manufacture their stuff." Scott was relieved that Armel was cooperating. He had feared a round of dick measuring and turf wars and had been dreading a confrontation.

"Most of the border with Canada isn't fenced or guarded. There are back roads that cross over with nothing but a warning sign. I've heard plenty of stories about hunters blundering into Canada chasing a deer or a moose," Armel said. "You honestly couldn't find a better place for people who were determined to slip through—especially if your coyotes can actually become coyotes."

"That's the problem. It's hard enough to catch people, but the Mounties can't go around arresting coyotes."

"That would attract attention," Armel agreed. "But you can't single-handedly hit every little burg in the forest. So what's the plan?"

"Good ol' shoe leather," Scott replied. "Talk to people, ask questions—sooner or later, someone has heard something."

"You sure they didn't send you out on a snipe hunt?" Armel asked. "These woods are big, largely unpopulated, and full of places someone who doesn't want to be found can hide. Damn near perfect for running contraband—which, by the way, people in these parts have been known to do for a couple hundred years, long before the Revolution."

Scott had wondered that himself when he realized how vast the territory was, but he trusted April and her crew not to put him through a hazing.

"They have psychics of their own back at headquarters. And this was where they wanted me to start. I guess it's up to me to find out why."

"I won't get in the way of your investigation, but I expect you to respect people's rights and property," Armel warned. "If you need backup, ask for it. And while I'll happily help you bust bad guys, I'm rather protective of the folks here so best be very sure before you point fingers."

Scott took the warning to heart, appreciating the offer of assistance. "I'd like to know if you hear any rumors or see anything strange. I realize this is a tourist area, and plenty of hikers and campers come through here, but the drug runners are going to want to pass their cargo off quickly to minimize their risk. So I guess if you see something strange, no matter how small, say something."

"Will do." Armel stood, signifying the end of their meeting, and shook Scott's hand with his big mitt. "Give my best to the boys in Albany."

BY THE TIME Scott got back to the Fox Hollow Lake Motel, it was time to get ready for his date with Gage. The butterflies in his stomach surprised him. While Scott hadn't dated anyone recently, he didn't usually get nervous just meeting someone for drinks and dinner.

This isn't just someone. This might be THE someone. I don't want to screw it up.

I probably shouldn't be going on a date while on a job. They didn't say I couldn't. And I have no reason to think Gage is doing anything wrong with his special brew. I don't think my taste magic would steer me wrong about him being my person if he was also a bad guy.

I haven't felt like this about someone in a long time. That's part of why I don't want to wait. I'm not just looking for a fun evening and a roll in the hay. I might not be a shifter, but I'd really like to find my mate.

When the taste of chocolate and strawberries came to his mouth again, Scott took that as a hopeful sign that things would work out.

Scott showered, making sure to manscape and clean thoroughly everywhere, just in case. He wasn't sure how far he wanted to take things tonight—or whether intimacy would even be on offer—but if the evening moved that way, he wanted to feel good about himself.

It's been a while. Too long. But I got tired of guys who just wanted a good time and no strings. Maybe I grew up or got old. I'm ready to find the right one.

He took time to comb his curls into some sort of style instead of just drying it and debated what to wear. Since he had packed for a variety of scenarios, he dug out a nice casual shirt and a dressy pair of jeans that showed off his ass.

Scott looked at himself in the mirror from all angles and let out a sigh. "That's as good as it's going to get. I hope he likes what he sees."

He felt as nervous as a high school date when he arrived at the Fox Hollow Hotel and stepped up to the dining room podium to be seated. When he didn't immediately see Gage, his heart sped up, although he highly doubted he was being ghosted.

"Hi." Gage slipped up beside him. "You're right on time." Gage slid his hand lightly across Scott's lower back as he stepped up and checked in for their reservation.

Gage looked good enough to eat in a black V-neck T-shirt and tight black jeans. He had primped a little as well, making it clear this was a real date and not just friends catching a bite to eat.

"I was worried about getting caught in traffic," Scott joked.

Gage grinned. "This winter, during the snowmobile rally, that might actually be a problem. Most days, no."

The host took them to a table in a quiet nook where they were out of the main traffic flow but could still see the small stage where a guitarist would be playing later in the evening.

"I like the vibe. Classy Victorian." Scott looked around. The restaurant managed to be formal but not stuffy with a rustic chic style that harkened back to the area's Gilded Age past.

"A hundred and fifty years ago, when the Vanderbilts and

their buddies came up here to their great camps, that made the area popular with the people who weren't in the robber baron class but wished they were," Gage replied. "Which fueled a boom in hotels like this and the Sagamore, among others, for the folks with aspirations."

"They weren't the only ones though." Scott remembered what he had read. "Plenty of people like to hunt and fish."

Gage nodded. "There are private lands throughout the area, many of them owned by regular people. And of course for Fox Hollow, the people who left Lily Dale after the scandal about the Fox Sisters turned this from an outpost into a real town."

Scott had read up on the area, and found the history fascinating. He was especially intrigued about how three sisters who had gained worldwide fame for being mediums had fallen from grace when their psychic abilities were questioned. No longer welcome in Lily Dale, a town famous for embracing Spiritualism, their followers had made the trek to what became Fox Hollow and opened the Fox Institute.

"That whole Spiritualist era is really interesting," Scott said. "I know that some people said it was all fake, but from what I've read, it seems like there were folks with real abilities who got painted with the same brush as the frauds."

He couldn't read the look in Gage's eyes, but then Gage nodded. "I agree. And the Fox Institute carries on the legacy, working to develop those authentic gifts. A lot of folks around here have some psychic ability. Whether or not people believe doesn't make their gifts less real."

They took a moment to study the menu. Scott's stomach growled, reminding him that lunch had been too long ago.

"All the food I've had here was good." Gage shifted so that their hands brushed. His knee bumped Scott's and stayed pressed against him, although they had plenty of room.

"What do you recommend?"

"I haven't had everything, but I've enjoyed all the stuff I've tried, and I've never heard that anyone got something they didn't like," Gage replied. "They're famous for their wings and steaks, but their pasta dishes are good, too. I don't want to be too full to move when we're done since the night's young."

His tone and the look in his eyes conveyed intent, and Scott smiled back, feeling himself chub at the possibilities.

"We can always burn off the calories." Scott hoped he hadn't forgotten how to flirt.

"Sounds good to me."

Scott ordered the Chicken Piccata, and Gage got the Chicken Scampi plus a bottle of Pinot Grigio.

The dinner crowd filled the empty tables, and a pleasant conversational buzz filled the room.

"So what brings you to Fox Hollow?" Gage asked. The tone was light, but Scott felt the weight of the words.

"I'm a food reviewer," he fell back on his cover, which had been the truth until a few weeks ago. He didn't want to lie to Gage, especially since he hoped they could hit it off, but he didn't know him well enough to share his secret. *I hope that we get close enough for me to tell him the whole truth. But I've already told Armel—so I can't wait too long.*

"I thought I'd catch up with one of my professors from Ithaca who relocated up here and do a foodie tour with reviews— working holiday." It was mostly true, but he still felt a pang of guilt.

I just got to town. I haven't done much yet to track down the bad guys. Blowing my cover so soon isn't going to help me catch the coyotes.

"Well, you've already hit the two best places in town—my taproom and the hotel," Gage joked. "But I'm happy to make recommendations about other good places in the area. We've got some amazing restaurants up here—when the cold sets in, people really value good food."

"I'd appreciate your suggestions," Scott replied. "I'm open to ideas." He kept eye contact longer than in a casual conversation and saw a spark in Gage's gaze that said the interest was mutual.

Scott asked more about how Gage came to start the taproom, sincerely interested and not as part of his cover. "That's quite a different path if all the rest of your family is military." He appreciated Gage's independence.

Gage sighed. "Yeah, I won't say that my choices always went over well, and I'm not as close to them as I used to be, but this was what I wanted to do, and I'm proud of how it turned out."

"How do you come up with the flavors? They're very original." Scott told himself he wasn't interviewing Gage as a suspect; instead, he hoped he could clear Gage so they could move on to other things without guilt.

"I go with what appeals to me, and people make requests," Gage said. "I've been working with beer one way or another for a while now. Some combinations are spectacularly bad, but others turn out even better than I hoped."

"Does it take a lot of exotic ingredients? You're not exactly in a metropolitan area to run to a specialty store." Scott held his breath, waiting for an answer.

"I keep things simple. Traditional formulas with a twist, local ingredients. Anything I can't get in Fox Hollow, I can usually get in Saranac Lake or Lake George. It doesn't pay to use ingredients that are too difficult to get because then they go out of stock or it makes the batch too expensive," Gage explained.

Scott let out a breath he didn't realize he was holding. Gage had no reason to lie to him. Unless Gage was psychic or had been tipped off—neither of which Scott thought was true—his answer placed him beyond suspicion. Relief made Scott's heart flutter. *I ran his name through the database, and it was clean. Good. Because I already know I want him.*

They flirted through dinner, brushing fingers, nudging knees, and dropping innuendos. Even so, they lingered over the meal, in no rush to see where the evening led. When the acoustic guitarist took his spot on the small stage, Gage and Scott dallied over a second glass of wine, fingers intertwined beneath the table.

"I've got this—this time." Gage picked up the tab. "You can do it next time. Because I'd really like us to have a next time."

"Me, too," Scott replied. "How's the rest of your week look?"

Gage chuckled. "You don't let any grass grow under your feet."

"Not when I see something I like." Scott surprised himself with his candor.

"How about dinner tomorrow night? We can talk about more places for your reviews, and if you're open during the day, we could go over to the Adirondack Museum. It's a pretty drive, and the exhibits are a must-see."

"I'd like that." Scott squeezed Gage's hand.

They walked back to where they had parked, and the tension crackled so hard between them Scott was surprised he couldn't see sparks. Neither of them had too much alcohol to drive, so the direction of the night hung in the balance.

"Want to come back to my cabin?" Gage offered. "I'm not ready to say goodnight yet."

"Neither am I." Scott was relieved that Gage had made the first move. His cramped motel room wasn't the ideal love nest.

"It's not far. Follow me," Gage said, and before Scott realized what was happening, Gage leaned in and kissed him on the cheek. "For luck." He winked.

"WELCOME TO MY HUMBLE ABODE." Gage bowed dramatically and swept out his arm when they got out of their cars in front of his cabin.

"Wow. This is great. I've only ever had apartments," Scott said.

The cabin was bigger than Scott expected, the size of a small house. The walls were logs, with cedar plank floors, and while it was not new, it had clearly been cared for lovingly.

"The place used to belong to my friend's uncle, and when he

decided he was too old to come up here anymore, he wanted to sell it to someone in the community," Gage said. "My friend recommended me, and I got lucky."

This doesn't sound like a guy who is going to risk blowing up everything to smuggle drugs, Scott thought. *He's already got what he wants, and he doesn't need the risk. Plus, he seems seriously invested in the community. He was a natural to be on my list to check, but they told me to trust my instincts, and I think Gage checks out—and not just because I want to sleep with him. SPAM can't fire me for having sex. James Bond did it all the time.*

"What do you like to watch?" Gage turned to him when they settled on the couch in front of the TV. "Sports? Movies? Got a favorite streaming show?"

Scott held his breath, hoping their chemistry and interests continued to align. "I like most things that are paranormal—ghosts, magic, that sort of thing. Not necessarily horror—just spooky. I hate to say it, but I'm not a big sports person, although I can enjoy a good game with the right people—and good tail-gating food."

"Then we're on the same page," Gage replied. "I'll admit, I have a weakness for shows about monster hunters, especially if the actors are hot."

That narrowed it down, and they found they shared a couple of favorite series. The night was still young with plenty of time to watch an episode from each and then decide where the evening should go.

"Do you want to spend the night?" Gage asked. "I can open another bottle of wine, and no one has to worry about driving."

Whether they continued binge-watching or moved to other pursuits, Scott welcomed the invitation. His motel room seemed cold and lonely, and he felt warm and welcome in Gage's cabin. "That sounds fantastic." *I hope he's who he seems to be. I'm really falling for this guy.*

Another glass of wine left them both relaxed but still barely buzzed. They moved closer together on the couch until they were sitting pressed together from knee to shoulder, fingers intertwined. When the credits rolled, Gage turned toward him.

"I want to kiss you—for real. Is that okay?"

"I've been wanting to kiss you all night," Scott confessed.

For a while, kisses and touching sufficed as they explored each other. Scott was already hard, and he could feel Gage's erection pressing against him through his jeans. Scott tasted chocolate and strawberries again. *Everything I've read says a recurring, sensuous taste is telling me this is someone special. A partner. A mate.*

Gage touched Scott with reverent possession, claiming and passionate. Nothing about his touch was hesitant, although he made sure Scott was on board with every shift.

"Are you okay with this?" Gage asked, letting his hands cup Scott's ass cheeks.

"Oh, yeah."

"There's no rush," Gage told him. "We don't have to do everything all at once. We have all the time in the world to do this right. I'm not going anywhere. We belong together."

Maybe it was their growing bond, but Scott felt like his body was an instrument being awakened to its best music by a maestro. That sounded dramatic, but he couldn't think of a better way to put into words what it felt like to be seduced by a lover who knew how to bring him pleasure and cared about making it memorable for both of them.

Scott didn't have extensive experience. Most encounters had been rushed fumbles when he was younger, neither of them really knowing what they were doing or how their bodies worked. When he got older, he had been left unsatisfied by lovers who didn't bother to make sure the release and satisfaction were mutual, who got too rough or showed a side of themselves during sex that turned Scott off.

Gage knew how to give pleasure. He licked and sucked at Scott's nipples until Scott almost thought he would come just from that. By the time Gage had worked his way down Scott's body to blow him, Scott was aching for release. Scott returned the favor, enjoying seeing Gage come apart and spill into his mouth.

They kissed and stroked until they were hard again, in no hurry for another climax, just enjoying getting to know one another at a whole different level. He mapped out Gage's sensitive spots, and Gage found the places where even a slight touch went straight to his balls. He discovered where Gage was ticklish and surrendered to Gage learning the same about him.

Scott tried to memorize Gage's body, every freckle and mole. He learned about the dog bite scar and the thin white line from a bike accident in middle school. Gage wanted to know about Scott's tattoo, and he had admitted it was a protection symbol borrowed from his favorite television show.

To Gage's credit, he hadn't laughed. Instead, he said that symbols held power because of belief in them, so it didn't matter about the source if Scott's intent was sincere.

Lying together afterward felt particularly intimate, talking about everything and nothing in the dark. Gage ran hot, so sleeping tangled up wasn't going to work, but the afterglow was peaceful and encouraged Scott's fantasy that Gage could be his forever person—his mate.

They hadn't fucked each other—yet—but they had checked off most of the other boxes, and Scott sensed they both were in favor of taking the next step. How far they went on their next date, he didn't know, but he realized that he had never felt as comfortable with someone as he did with Gage.

He and Gage were easy together, something Scott hadn't experienced often, and he didn't feel judged or measured. They liked many of the same things, so conversation didn't take effort.

Gage was hot in an adorably nerdy way, even better because he seemed confident and didn't swagger. They had a combustible sexual attraction, but Scott sensed that Gage was looking for more than a hot roll in the hay.

He doesn't seem like a guy who plays the field. Maybe he would like to find a forever guy, too. Am I being fair to let this move forward? He doesn't know the truth about what I do—and I can't tell him, at least not for a while. Would SPAM let me work remotely? Gage can't relocate his taproom, and he loves living in Fox Hollow. It wouldn't be fair to ask him to give that up. I think I could fall in love with living here too.

I don't think he's in on the smuggling, but I do get the sense there's something he isn't telling me. Then again, I haven't told him everything either. It's early days—we have a lot of getting to know each other to do, and I've got a case to solve. Telling the sheriff and Dr. Jeffries was one thing. And I'll tell Gage before I tell anyone else. But not yet.

I'm sure he's some sort of paranormal. He's not a strong psychic, but I pick up some ability. There's something more, but I don't recognize the feel of it.

Scott had read the brief on Fox Hollow before he left Albany. By all accounts, the Fox Institute was well-regarded and above reproach with a sterling reputation and finding that Dr. Jeffries was on faculty there was a real bonus.

As for the rest of the town, reports said that it offered a safe place for shifters of all kinds, and as long as everyone played nicely together, SPAM didn't seem inclined to intervene. He suspected that people with other special abilities might have also found a haven there. Scott also got the impression that SPAM's intel about such things might not be widely shared with other, less tolerant, government agencies.

Scott had no desire to bring the wrong sort of feds down on what seemed like a truly lovely town.

He thought about the tasting at the taproom. He had come to Fox Hollow looking for clues to a smuggling operation and instead found a man who might be his fated mate if you believed in that sort of thing. And Scott did, deep down.

At the same time, there was something paranormal about Gage and his brews that Scott couldn't define. He had some experience with psychics, but he didn't sense that to be Gage's thing.

Is he a shifter? How would I know if I don't see him change? He seems happily settled here in Fox Hollow. Not exactly the type to throw in his lot with smugglers and drug runners. I like him. Maybe too much. We have a connection — is it enough to build on? That's jumping ahead a lot after just a few days, but we're both old enough to know what we want.

Could it work? Or is there some nefarious connection I haven't spotted yet? I hope not. I think I could fall for Gage — even more than I already have.

CHAPTER 6
SCOTT

Scott woke up with Gage snuggled close behind him. The hard length of Gage's cock pressed against the cleft of Scott's ass. His dick was definitely on board with the possibilities.

"Good morning," Gage purred. "In the mood for a *really* good wake-up call?"

Scott shifted to face Gage and kissed him. "Oh, yeah. I'm not usually a morning person, but I think you could change my mind."

They made out with unhurried passion, taking their time to climax. Hand jobs and frot with plenty of pre-come and some lube made for a sleepy, sensual way to start the morning. Scott paid attention to how Gage's eyes fluttered closed when they kissed and the quiet moans he made when Scott's fingers found just the right spots.

Everything about Gage seemed different than Scott's previous boyfriends. Gage had made clear that he wanted Scott, but he didn't try to dominate. Even after they had established that they both wanted sex, Gage remained solicitous and checked before moving forward, still respectful. The more time

Scott spent with Gage, the clearer it was in his mind that Gage could be the one for him.

Now if we can just get past the secrets.

If Gage was a shifter, then the only ones who didn't know were mundanes and out-of-towners—like Scott.

How long will it take him to trust me? And how soon can I feel right about telling him about SPAM? We've covered a lot of ground in a short time. He cleared the database. That means he's okay.

Which of us will break the standoff first? I'll feel better telling him my secret once I know his. Maybe he feels the same way. I guess we could try blurting it out at the same time, but that seems juvenile.

When they finished making love, Gage wiped them down with his sleep shirt. "Go ahead and take the first shower, and I'll get breakfast going."

By the time Scott came out of the bathroom, he smelled bacon and found Gage plating freshly cooked bacon and hot toaster waffles.

"The maple syrup is real Canadian stuff," he told Scott. Gage's hair stood out at odd angles, and Scott thought he looked adorable.

"This looks fantastic." Scott's stomach rumbled.

Gage put the plates on the table while Scott poured coffee for both of them. They dug in and polished off the food in record time.

"What's the plan for today? Part of my assignment is getting to know the area, so if you still want to do the museum and diner again, I'm completely up for it." Scott grinned. "Honestly, I'm up for anything if it involves hanging out together."

"I need to go into the taproom and make sure everything is going okay. No one has called off, that sort of thing. Want to meet there at ten? You can park out back, and I can drive," Gage offered.

"Sounds good to me. And your breakfast was fantastic."

Gage looked pleased. "Got to keep giving you reasons to keep coming back."

"You give me plenty of reasons to keep coming," Scott grinned.

After breakfast, Scott and Gage parted after a long, gentle, surprisingly passionate kiss in the driveway. While Gage's cabin was not in view of the road, Scott took his willingness to kiss out in the open as a good sign. He'd had too many boyfriends who treated their relationship like a dirty little secret, which told him either the guy wasn't as out as he claimed or he wasn't as monogamous as he pretended. Once again, Gage effortlessly passed a test Scott didn't realize he had raised.

How can I feel so much for him when we've only known each other such a short time? I'm not bewitched—the SPAM charms would tell me when I put them back on. Is this what it really feels like to find the right one?

SCOTT STOPPED for coffee and a donut at the Black Bear Café. He noted that the owner bore a strong resemblance to Sheriff Armel and asked if they were related.

"Yep—I'm his sister. Welcome to Fox Hollow. It's a small world."

From there, once he had finished his snack, Scott headed to the library. He recognized the slim, red-haired man at the front desk from RPG Night at Gage's taproom.

"Welcome. I'm Liam, the head librarian. How can I help you?"

Scott smiled, hoping he looked like a tourist. "Hi, I'm new in town, and I'm looking for maps. I'd like to do some hikes and get to know the area."

Liam looked him over like he remembered seeing him before, and Scott wondered whether Liam and Gage knew each other well.

"Yes, we have maps," Liam replied. "Before I show you where, let me give you my spiel. These are forever wild woods.

They are vast, and there are big areas without houses, roads—or good cell signal. People get lost. Some people are never found." Liam gave him a pointed look.

"Don't leave the trail. Always make sure someone knows where you're going and when you plan to get back. There are wild animals out there. Some of them eat people. Avoid those. Don't be out after dark. Take a map and a compass—and make sure you know how to use it. Thank you for coming to my TED talk."

"Sounds like you've said all that before," Scott replied.

"More than you know. Are you looking for something in particular?" Liam asked.

"I want to go up to the fire tower. Wondering if you can see Canada from there."

"Nope. Common misconception," Liam answered. "But it's a very pretty view if you don't mind all those steps."

Scott left with photos and photocopies of the maps and promised Liam he would take safety precautions. He already had good hiking boots, sunscreen, bug spray, a hat, and legit outdoor clothing, as well as several bottles of water and a compass in his bag.

It's just a short hike, he told himself, although he appreciated Liam's cautions. He drove to the trail nearest the fire tower and put a note with the time he left and his objective on the dashboard visible through the windshield. That way, if something kept him from coming back for the car in a reasonable time, the ranger would know how long he had been gone and where he was headed.

The woods smelled of pine and wet dirt, and the rustle of the branches overhead made Scott smile remembering other times outdoors growing up or with friends. Once he got to college, free time became more limited. He couldn't remember how long it had been since he last went for a hike without a deadline to return.

Scott also carried bear spray, something he thought was a

joke when he first heard about it. *Sure, I'll take that the next time I go clubbing,* he had thought. But when he read up on the dangers of hiking in deep woods, he changed his mind. If he did attract the wrong sort of attention, the spray was likely to protect him more than the Glock in its holster under his jacket.

His approach sent birds flying from their branches and small animals scurrying into the underbrush. Scott's suburban life in Albany seemed like a world away. He knew that the region's native settlers had lived in these woods, and later, the Gilded Era's rich built massive great camps that melded the wilderness with Manhattan chic. But except for the towns that dotted the few highways, no houses ringed the lakes or marred the peaks.

Forever wild meant something out here.

Scott heard a noise and froze. He turned in a slow circle, worried he might be on the menu for one of the forest's wild residents. A few dozen feet away stood a majestic moose with a full rack of antlers. The huge animal stared at him with expressive, dark eyes as if it had been looking for him, then craned its neck and stripped leaves from a nearby branch.

He had seen plenty of white-tailed deer over the years, but nothing prepared him for how massive the moose was, how tall it stood, or how wide its antlers were. "Wow. It must take a lot of leaves to fill you up," he said to the moose, who stopped munching long enough to stare back.

Scott took it as a good sign that the moose seemed to be relaxed. That probably meant there weren't predators around big enough to be a threat. Still, he stayed alert, watching and listening as he headed to the top of the lookout tower.

The view from the platform took his breath away. He might not be able to see all the way to Canada, but it sure seemed like it with forest spreading all around. Scott was still trying to wrap his mind around how big the Adirondacks were, and now he felt even more impressed. Lakes, mountains, forests, and clearings filled the vista. In the distance, he heard a raptor's cry.

I think I know why people like to live here. It would take some getting used to in the winter, but it sure is pretty.

He climbed down after a while, being extremely cautious on the metal stairs. As he neared the bottom, Scott spotted a big black dog with large, pointed ears just before it faded into the shadows beneath the trees. The taste of chocolate and strawberries filled his mouth, and Scott wondered about the timing and whether it meant anything.

Was that a wolf? It didn't look quite right. Maybe I can scare it away.

Scott pulled out his phone, cued up music, and raised the volume as high as it would go. Just to be safe, he grabbed a large stick, although he wasn't sure what good it would do if the moose or the big dog decided to attack.

Neither animal made a move to come closer, but they both followed him all the way back to the parking lot before slipping away under the trees.

That was weird. Did they expect me to feed them?

Scott leaned against the car and ate a trail bar, washing it down with a bottle of water. Other than having a nice outing and getting a little exercise, he was no closer to finding the drug smugglers than before he left town.

If they really are coyote shifters, I'll never spot them in all these trees. And if they're people, it's still a massive territory, especially if they don't stick to the main trails. Scott's heart sank. *My first assignment isn't going great. I might wash out before I even get a chance to prove myself.*

Scott thought about what he had seen and realized it seemed unlikely that anyone was using the watch tower as a drug drop. Nothing around it looked recently disturbed, and he didn't get any psychic nudge via a strange taste in his mouth that he had found a clue, except the strawberries and chocolate that until now he had associated with Gage.

Back to the drawing board. Maybe the tower was too notable a landmark—and too easy for other people to blunder into finding a drop.

When I go back to the library, I'll look at the maps again and see if I can pick up on other possible rendezvous spots that are out of the way but easy to spot. I doubt the drug makers would be happy if their shipments got left by the wrong tree in the forest.

And what about that big dog and the moose? I tasted chocolate and strawberries—like when I'm with Gage. Is Gage a shifter? If so, which one was he? As soon as he thought the question, Scott knew the answer. *Gage was the guard dog. It fits him.*

Did Liam call Gage to tell him I was poking around in the woods? Was I being protected or watched? And who was the moose?

How do I know if I'm being followed by shifters? I'm going to start looking at every alley cat suspiciously.

As he drove back to town, Scott found himself questioning his assignment. He knew his superiors were worried about people being harmed by inferior or poisonous concoctions or fake medicines that didn't provide a remedy. Mundane law enforcement certainly had their hands full trying to control the flow of illegal, addictive drugs and shut down those networks.

But Dr. Jeffries had a point about the need for altered medications and legal recreational drugs suited to supernatural metabolisms. To Scott, that wasn't different from people needing different dosages due to weight or body size. If the human manufacturers couldn't provide those alternatives because the supernatural world was hidden, what option was there except for parallel suppliers to step in to meet a very real need?

Scott thought back to the taproom with Gage. He enjoyed the creative brews, but he had noted an unusual aftertaste that tingled a bit like magic. At the time, his focus was on flirting with Gage since Scott had been off-duty.

Now, he wondered if there was more to it. *This is a town full of shifters and probably other types of people with paranormal gifts whose systems don't work like mundanes. Has Gage figured out a way to brew beer that tastes good to regular people but packs more of a punch for supernaturals?*

That isn't illegal if no one is getting sick. Alcoholic beverages have a wide acceptable range of strengths. As long as he isn't using controlled substances to add more bang for the buck, it doesn't break any laws. And it would make so much sense if Gage was also a shifter.

By the time Scott got back to town, he realized it was almost time to meet up with Gage. He stopped for coffee and ducked into the restroom to untangle his hair and splash his face. He picked up another coffee for Gage and headed to the taproom.

Gage came out from the back office and greeted him with a grin. "Right on time. And is that for me?" he asked when Scott held out the second coffee, made the way he had observed Gage liked.

"Absolutely is," Scott confirmed.

Gage took a sip and gave a positively pornographic moan of happiness that went right to Scott's balls. His mischievous grin told Scott Gage knew exactly what he was doing.

"It's great—thank you. And you got it just right," Gage said.

"I'll do a lot to get you to make that noise again," Scott teased in a low voice, although there weren't many people in the taproom at this hour.

"Promise?" Gage asked with all kinds of mischief in his eyes.

Gage drove the short distance to Blue Mountain Lake on one of the prettiest stretches of road Scott had ever seen. At one point, they picked up fast food and ate at a roadside overlook.

"It's really beautiful up here."

"Yeah, there are a lot of roads like that up here," Gage said. "Sometimes you just want to pull over and stare. Especially in the fall when the leaves change. No wonder the photographers and leaf peepers descend in droves."

They held hands in the car as they drove, and Scott marveled at the brightly colored leaves spread across the mountains.

"It's pretty here in every season, but in fall, it really shows off," Gage agreed.

They talked about everything and nothing on the drive— high school memories, Gage's love for beer and why he opted out of his family's military tradition, and Scott's history as a food reviewer.

Scott was already planning a feature on "Fox Hollow Foodies" for one of his regular magazines. "It probably won't run until spring, but that's not too bad since I imagine there's a lot of snow up here in the winter."

Gage laughed. "Some years more than others, but yeah. Great for cross-country skiing, and there's a big snowmobile rally that ends in Fox Hollow. Ice fishing for the dedicated outdoors types. And the folks around town are pretty good at coming up with ways to stay amused all winter long." He waggled an eyebrow, which managed to put a salacious spin on his words.

The more Scott heard about Fox Hollow, the more he wanted to move there. Being with Gage would be fantastic, but everything he was hearing suggested that the town could be the sort of community he had always longed for.

They wandered through the museum, taking in the history of the area from the time of early trappers through the elaborate Victorian hotels to modern-day vacationers and sports players.

"I love the fancy train car that brought rich folks up from New York City," Scott said. Despite being over a century old, the car was opulently appointed.

"There were really big hotels like the Sagamore for those folks and some others that burned down over the years," Gage said. "The Fox Hollow Hotel is the more middle-class version."

"It's hard to imagine all those Victorian wealthy folks coming up here and pretending to get back to nature," Scott remarked.

"Some of them legitimately got into the hunting and fishing." Gage shrugged. "The others just came to party and figured they were roughing it because they had to leave their mansions."

Gage pointed out trivia about the exhibits that wasn't on the signs and admitted that he went to the museum several times a year for their seasonal displays. "It's a nice, peaceful way to clear my head, and the drive isn't too long. Of course, no one goes anywhere if there's a weather warning."

Scott understood. "How does that work in Fox Hollow when there's a bad storm?"

Gage shrugged as if the question had an obvious answer. "Everyone pulls together. Some of the more vulnerable people come to the motels so they can be looked after. We've got a pretty good emergency response team for extreme weather, and people pay attention and help each other. Part of what I love about the place."

They spent several hours wandering the exhibits, but Scott knew they could come back again and again and always see something new. Gage took him to dinner at a fantastic little restaurant run by a former big city chef.

"This place is awesome," Scott said. "I'm going to need to come back just to write about it."

After dinner, they walked along the lake's beach before heading back to Gage's cabin.

"Thank you for an amazing day." Scott and Gage held hands on the front seat, and Scott couldn't remember feeling more at peace.

"It's all part of a nefarious plot to get you to move closer." Gage squeezed Scott's hand.

"Your plot is succeeding," Scott told him. "I haven't put down any roots in Albany, and I can work from anywhere." He sincerely hoped SPAM would agree.

"Fox Hollow gets busy with tourists from the time the snow melts in the spring until it gets deep in the fall," Gage told him. "Even then, the visits slow down, but they don't stop because we get the skiers, snowshoers, ice fishing fans, winter camping—a whole lot of cold stuff that isn't my thing," he added with a chuckle.

"I like staying warm and sharing body heat." Scott leaned into Gage.

"I like that too," Gage replied.

They came back to the cabin and headed inside. "I know that

was an awesome dinner, but I've got snacks if we get peckish later. Want to crash on the couch and watch something?" Gage asked.

"Sounds perfect to me."

When is the right time to tell him about SPAM? I've had that chocolate-strawberry taste all day, and I hope my taste magic wouldn't have me falling for a guy I need to send to jail. But Gage hasn't spilled his secret yet, either. Was he one of the animals I saw this morning? He doesn't strike me as the moose type. The big black dog? Maybe. But when will he trust me enough to tell me?

They spent the rest of the evening curled up together watching reruns of their favorite buddy flick monster hunting show. Both of them had seen it enough to quote lines and watch for bloopers, which removed all the tension from even the scariest episodes.

Scott let Gage take the lead in bed that night, and instead of escalating to anal, as Scott expected, Gage focused on touching and kissing, bringing them both off with another good hand job.

"I had a great day today," Scott said in a sleepy, sexed-out voice when they snuggled afterward. "Thank you."

"I have an ulterior motive," Gage joked. "I don't want you to go back to Albany. I'm hoping you'll love Fox Hollow enough to move closer." Unspoken was the *and me* that Scott picked up as clearly as if it had been said aloud.

"I'll put in a request when I go back." Scott kissed him. "You make a very persuasive case."

After a very satisfying round of blow jobs and a breakfast of toast and maple link sausage, Scott kissed Gage goodbye with the promise of having dinner together again that night.

Scott felt a tug on his heart as he drove away and thought again about how quickly the bond between them had formed.

I'm not a shifter. Can I have a mate bond? But I'm pretty sure Gage is, so if he feels the bond, it would affect me too, right?

He liked the idea of a mystical connection that elevated their romance to something destined. *I'm a hopeless romantic. Now I just have to hope that confessing my secret identity to Gage won't ruin everything.*

Lying in bed that morning, Scott had tried to get up the courage but didn't want to blurt his news without thinking about how best to admit his real reason for being in town.

Dr. Jeffries and the sheriff were right—I should have said something before this. But it's only been days, not like I've let things drag on for weeks. And I've ruled out more than I've ruled in on my case. I might not have to get SPAM's permission to relocate at this rate. They might just fire me, and I'll be back to depending on food reviews to pay the rent.

Scott drove back to the Fox Hollow library after stopping for a coffee and drinking it in the car. His heart still fluttered after the morning with Gage, and he couldn't stop thinking about how good they were together. Despite having just left the cabin, Scott couldn't wait for their dinner date that night.

I'm going to have to bite the bullet and tell him the truth about SPAM. If we're meant to be, it won't matter. And then maybe he'll trust me enough to own up to being a shifter. Because I'm sure he was the big black dog in the woods. Good thing I'm not allergic.

Scott headed to the library, where Liam waved from behind the main desk.

"Did you find the fire tower?" Liam asked.

"Yes, thank you. Great view. And spotted some very inter-esting wildlife on the way," Scott said.

Liam didn't even blink. "Plenty of that around these parts. Just steer clear of the ones that will eat you."

"Do you have any more in-depth maps of the area between here and the border? Government reports, aerial surveys, that sort of thing?" Scott asked.

"Can I ask what you're trying to find? Because otherwise you could have a mountain of stuff and none of it the right thing," Liam replied.

"I think it would be fun to do some articles on backroads food finds," Scott replied. That was certainly something he had thought about as a set of articles he might pitch to regional magazines, but not the only reason for wanting the surveys.

"Well, there are plenty of those," Liam agreed. "But some of those resources are restricted, so I need to photocopy your driver's license to let you check them out."

"Sure," Scott said and took out his wallet. When he slid his license out, his SPAM ID fell on the floor.

"You dropped this," Liam held onto it just long enough that Scott was sure Liam had read the card. If so, Liam didn't let on, although his smile seemed a bit more fixed. "Here's your official Fox Hollow library card." Liam signed the back of a card he printed from the front desk computer. "Those books have different lending rules, so please bring them back in three days."

"I will. And thanks for the library card." Scott gathered his resources and headed back to his motel room. To Scott's relief, everything was just as he left it, although he had barely spent any time inside over the last few days.

He knew it was silly, but he missed Gage already. Scott remembered their morning lovemaking and how comfortable he felt in Gage's arms.

I never believed in the whole fated mates thing before, but I really hope it's true. I want that with Gage. More than anything. I just have to finish my mission and see if I can relocate. Then we can be together. And if SPAM doesn't work out, maybe I can come up with a cool tapas menu for Gage's bar.

Scott made another cup of coffee from the in-room carafe and settled in at the table.

He studied the maps and consulted the internet, looking for likely hand-off spots for smugglers. The longer he was in Fox

Hollow, the more he concluded that the drug runners would be stupid to try to base their operation nearby. Not only would the locals recognize them as shifters, but the psychics would catch on quickly, and depending on the range of supernatural abilities possessed by the townspeople, the coyotes might find themselves magically outgunned.

If you can't beat them, join them. Maybe I've been wrong keeping why I'm here a secret. I'll ask Dr. Jeffries what he thinks, but perhaps if I ask for help, the townspeople might be willing to share what they know. After all, they've got a lot at stake since this is their home. They don't want drug runners around, either. And if there's a blurry line between helpful medications fine-tuned for special metabolisms and dangerous drugs, maybe I can take that information back to SPAM—without outing my sources—and make the case that not all altered substances are bad.

Scott was new at SPAM, but he hoped it wasn't naïve to think that his input might be listened to and considered. If the organization truly wanted to protect people with supernatural abilities as well as stop paranormal threats, helping them get medicine and de-stressors that worked seemed like a reasonable accommodation.

Scott showered and changed, getting ready for his date. He found himself looking forward to having dinner with Gage even more than before, and although everything had been going well so far, Scott still felt nervous.

Are we going to go to the next level? Or do we need to take this slow? I'm going to try to take my cue from him because I already know I want all of him all the time. Maybe even forever.

He looked at himself in the mirror, trying to tame an errant curl. Scott checked himself from all sides as best he could, annoyed at the small bathroom mirror that didn't give him a full-length reflection. He wasn't vain, but he wanted to look good for his lover.

Lover. I like the sound of that.

Just thinking about Gage gave him a taste of chocolate and strawberries, the taste of romance—and true love.

I really hope things work out for us. Even if I have to quit being a secret agent after just getting started, if he and I really are true mates, I'd do that. I've wanted someone of my own for a long time.

Scott didn't have a great track record when it came to love. More than once, a boyfriend's ambition put a stop to the relationship when constant long hours or a major relocation caused friction. Some connections fizzled, while other former partners hadn't been ready to stop playing the field. Scott had enjoyed his carefree dating years, but now that he was in his thirties, the idea of having a special someone to settle down with took on greater appeal.

With Gage, everything seemed to fall into place. They felt right together, despite it still being early in their relationship. Scott liked that he felt so comfortable with Gage, even though he hadn't yet trusted him with the full story.

I'll tell him everything tonight and beg forgiveness. I haven't lied— I just haven't told the whole truth. He winced at the thought, knowing he was playing semantic games. Withholding information—even if there were government restrictions on what he could share—could still be viewed as a form of dishonesty.

I'm sure I don't know everything about him, either. We're still in the discovery phase, learning about each other. That's how it goes; sharing little bits as the trust builds. At least, that's how I always thought it should work. Maybe once I share, he'll admit that he's a shifter.

Scott picked a dark green shirt that brought out his eyes and dabbed a bit of cologne on his neck. The curls couldn't be entirely tamed, but short of washing and drying his hair again, he doubted it could be fixed.

Sooner or later we won't see each other at our best. If what we have is real, it should be strong enough to deal with that. At least, that's what Scott hoped in his hopelessly romantic heart of hearts.

When he went to the taproom, Scott didn't see Gage behind

the bar or circulating among the customers. Figuring that his date probably stepped out to get ready for their dinner, Scott went to get a drink and ordered one of the proprietary brews he hadn't had before.

He looked around as he waited for the bartender to pour for him. Every table in the taproom was taken, and he had snagged one of the last seats at the bar. That meant Gage's brewery was doing well, and Scott was happy for him.

I wonder how many of the people here have extra abilities? Are they shifters? It's not dark out yet, so probably not vampires. Would witches react differently to medicine? How about were-creatures?

Scott's supernatural education with SPAM had just begun, so he suspected that there were many other types of paranormal creatures out there about which he knew nothing. Or, if what he did know came from television, he accepted that most of it was probably wrong.

The world is a bigger, stranger place than I ever suspected.

His intuition pinged a little when Gage showed up exactly on time, not a moment early. Scott had arrived nearly twenty minutes early, not worried about seeming too eager. Now he wondered if that was a mistake.

I was never into playing hard to get. If you have to play games, it's not a forever relationship. That sort of cat-and-mouse might be fun on a lark, but I don't want to spend the rest of my life constantly figuring out what the rules are and where I stand.

"Hi," Scott said. "You've got a good crowd tonight. This is a busy place." He meant it as a compliment that Gage's bar was doing well. He wasn't sure how his comment registered with Gage, who didn't respond.

"Sorry I'm late. It's been crazy in the back." His voice sounded flatter than usual, and something didn't quite reach his eyes.

"That's okay—there's a lot going on." Scott raised his beer. "I tried a new one. I really like it."

When Scott sipped the beer, he got strong impressions of Gage —his enthusiasm for coming up with new recipes, his commitment to the taproom, and his love for brewing. Gage's emotions infused the drink for Scott, turning into a savory language of insights.

From that, Scott felt even more sure that he and Gage were emotionally connected, a linked pair—something that was both thrilling and scary. He regretted not telling Gage the full truth up front.

Isn't that a theme in secret agent stories? Not knowing who to trust. A lot of the authors of those famous books had been real spies back in the day.

"Glad you like it," Gage replied. He seemed stiffer than before, more reserved, and something in his voice sent a warning.

"Is everything okay?" Scott didn't need a premonition to sense that their easy rapport had changed.

"We don't want to be late for our reservation," Gage said with a strained smile. "Come on. I'm starving."

Scott knew something was wrong. Gage seemed locked down, holding himself closely, not as gregarious and spontaneous as before. Scott wracked his brain to figure out why.

I showed up on time. I made an effort to look good. I asked about his day. He's pulled back, and he's angry. Oh, shit. He knows.

Scott went cold all over as he realized that someone—probably Liam—had spilled his secret. He didn't think it was malicious gossip. Liam probably wanted to warn his friend that Scott wasn't what he seemed, protecting him from disappointment. Scott could understand the impulse.

At the same time, it took away his chance to break the news when the time was right, now that they had built up trust and had reached a point when the admission made sense.

How do I salvage this? I don't want to lose him. Not over this. Scott decided to bite the bullet. *Either we'll work through this, or we won't. Maybe it's better to rip off the Band-Aid and see where the chips fall.* He had utterly mangled several metaphors, but he didn't care.

"Before we go, can we talk somewhere in private, please?" Scott did everything he could think of to make sure his body language and tone weren't aggressive.

"Yeah, I think that might be a good idea." Gage signaled the bartender. "Put his drink on my tab." He motioned for Scott to follow him.

Scott felt like a freshman headed for the principal's office as he trailed Gage to the back. They hadn't known each other long, and Scott didn't make a habit of rushing into relationships, but he had already begun to fall hard for Gage, something he chalked up to being fated mates.

If he's heard that I'm a secret agent from someone else, this isn't going to go well. I didn't mean to mislead him. But it's not going to look good.

"You can drop the act," Gage said when his office door shut behind them.

"What act?"

"The one where you pretend to like me so you can get info for your case. Was making out with me part of your investigation?" Gage sounded hurt and angry.

Scott felt like he'd been punched. "No. Of course not. Please —let me explain."

"Why should I believe you?"

"You've got a town full of psychics. If you don't believe what I tell you, have one of them read my mind or do a lie-detector thing. Hell, ask Dr. Jeffries or the sheriff. They already know."

Gage crossed his arms over his chest. He reminded Scott of a grim guard dog. "Start talking."

"I really am a food reviewer," Scott began. "Have been for several years. My magazine shut down, and I applied for jobs. I don't just like food—I have a minor psychic ability where I get a taste in my mouth as a clue to something important." *You taste like chocolate and strawberries and mate. But maybe I've blown that for good.* "I got hired by this place called SPAM—"

"Like the canned ham or the email?"

Scott sighed. "Neither. It's Special Processing And Management. They said I'd get that a lot."

"Go on." If Gage were a dog and gave him that look, Scott would expect to be bitten.

"It's a secret organization that recruits people with minor paranormal abilities to stop bad guys and save the world since the usual players—FBI, Secret Service, US Marshals—don't officially know about the supernatural." Those organizations actually had secret paranormal branches, but Scott was trying to keep things simple.

"So you're a spy?"

Scott winced. "More of a rookie secret agent or investigator. Someone is cooking up unregulated pharmaceuticals and recreational drugs adjusted for faster supernatural metabolisms. Since there's no way to regulate the trade without cluing the wider government in on the existence of paranormal creatures, the problem becomes making sure the products are safe and keeping the cartels out of the trade."

"So you just happened to show up in Fox Hollow?" Gage's voice was cold.

"SPAM sent me here—probably because of the Fox Institute. As it turned out, Dr. Jeffries at the Institute was one of my professors when I was in college in Ithaca. I thought he might be a good starting point." Scott wished he had told Gage when they first met, but that sort of undercut the whole secret part of secret agent, and he hadn't known who to trust.

"Keep going."

"When I checked in at the motel and asked for a recommendation, they told me your beer was really good. That's how I ended up here the first night."

"Am I a suspect? I develop beer recipes that affect people with paranormal metabolisms." Gage was still clearly pissed. "I don't use illegal substances. Everything is locally sourced, so nothing is smuggled from Canada, and there aren't any laws that prohibit the mixtures. I just think it's nice that shifters, vamps, and weres can grab a beer and get a little buzzed. Is that a crime?"

"No. Of course not. And the first night, when I met you at the taproom, I was on my own time, not investigating. I realized your name was on my list of people to check out—but by then, we had already met and hit it off. And I didn't want to ruin it. I still have my mission. There are bad guys bringing in dangerous drugs, and I need to catch them. As I told the sheriff, what they are pushing is a direct threat to the people who live in Fox Hollow. I'm not the enemy."

"You weren't honest with me."

Scott sighed. "I'm still new at the whole SPAM thing, but that's the secret part of being an undercover agent. I was planning to tell you. I hadn't expected to fall for you. When I met you, I got a taste of strawberries and chocolate in my mouth, and my mind took that as a sign." Scott figured that if he was going to lose Gage, he might as well lose big.

"A sign of what?"

"That you were my mate." Scott looked down, not wanting to see the rejection in Gage's eyes.

"Mate?"

"I know we're just getting to know each other," Scott said. "And I don't know how it works for you—I'm guessing that when I saw a dog and a moose on my trip to the fire tower, one of those was you?"

"Yeah, me and Brandon. I'm the Malinois. He's the moose. Liam said you were going out there, and we wanted to make sure you were safe."

"And keep an eye on what I was doing?"

Gage had the good grace to look a little chagrined. "Yeah, maybe. Like you said—we're all trying to figure this out. New guy comes to town, doesn't seem to be showing all his cards, starts looking at maps and asking questions. Can't blame us for being careful—since there have been rumors of smugglers. They seem to know to steer clear of Fox Hollow, but who knows if that will last?"

"I'm sorry," Scott said. "I honestly do like you—a lot. I think we could be good together. I never lied to you; I just didn't tell you the whole truth. I was going to once I got my bearings and figured out what was going on. I didn't mean to hurt you." He thought about pointing out that Gage hadn't told him about being a shifter but didn't think that would help.

"Yeah, well," Gage grumbled. "Look, I'd like some time to process. I'm not breaking things off, but my head is all over the place right now, and I need to think. So let's take the night off and postpone our dinner. We'll talk tomorrow. I promise I'll call you."

"Okay. Fair enough. Thanks for discussing it. I'll see you around." Scott needed space, and he didn't want to show how deeply disappointed he felt. He headed for the door, and Gage let him leave.

Scott managed not to look back. He hoped his expression didn't betray him as he walked out of the taproom, glad for once that he didn't know most people.

He got to his SUV and sat there for several minutes. Going back to his room right now would be awful. He remembered that the Fox Hollow Hotel had live music. Scott drove from the taproom over to the hotel and found a parking spot, figuring that he could walk back to the motel if he got too buzzed.

Scott found his way to the bar. A singer with a guitar played in the corner, and Scott paused to listen since he liked the song and the guy had a good voice. He made his way to the counter, surprised that with live entertainment there were seats open.

"You got lucky," the bartender said. "Some guy just got up and walked away. His loss—your win."

Scott ordered a whiskey and turned halfway so he could watch the singer. For now, he tried not to think about the conversation with Gage or how hurt he felt. He didn't want to examine anything too closely.

The bartender slid his drink across the counter, and Scott put down cash, including a generous tip. He focused on the music. The singer had a good voice and a mellow hits playlist of favorites.

Scott took a sip and let the whiskey burn down his throat. *This sort of thing never happened to James Bond. I didn't intend to be a superhero. It would be nice to do something useful with my ability, but I'm hardly likely to save the world. Who am I kidding? I'm not cut out for this kind of thing. Once this case is over, I'll call April and resign.*

I wish I was plain old normal, no super senses, no psychic stuff. It's never done me any good, and now it might cost me Gage, just when we were starting to hit it off.

The thought made him sad. Moving had been jarring, and he hadn't even had time to adjust to his new city before his new employer sent him out of town.

Everything I own is in a tiny apartment in Albany, but there wasn't anything for me in Rochester anyhow. If I quit SPAM, I can find something to do for a living that doesn't involve busting illegal drugs and criminals. Maybe I can get Dr. Jeffries to explain to Gage and he'll forgive me. I could move to Fox Hollow and start my own food blog and travel all around the area writing about cool restaurants. I could make special food for Gage's taproom or save up for a food truck. I hope Gage will give me another chance. I think we'd be good together.

Scott frowned as he picked up a strange taste, musky with a hint of Limburger cheese, that didn't come from the cocktail. When he looked down the bar, he saw a man who looked scruffy even by camper standards.

The stranger had a lean, rough look to him, more motorcycle gang than trail hiker. Scott figured that plenty of riders came through this way as well as outdoorsmen and looked around to see if there was a club represented, going on a group ride. He didn't see anyone else in leathers but reminded himself that many enthusiasts didn't dress the part.

The singer's repertoire was good for his range, an easy-listening mix of oldies and newer music that appealed to a wide audience. Scott mentally sang along to the next tune, surprised he knew all the words.

When he looked back, the tough guy was gone.

"Thought I might find you here." Liam slid into the seat next to Scott. He flagged the bartender and ordered a whiskey sour.

"I thought you had a Library Night or something over at the taproom." Scott figured Liam had blown his cover to Gage, but he couldn't find it in himself to be angry with him. *It's my fault. I should have handled it better.*

"That's tomorrow night. I hope you can make it. We usually have a lot of fun."

Scott appreciated the offer, but he knew that if he and Gage couldn't sort things out, he would be avoiding the taproom and leaving town as soon as possible.

"Thanks, but I need to find what I'm looking for," Scott replied. "Got a job to do."

Liam studied his drink for a few moments. "We're a protective bunch around here. Tourists come and go, but the locals are year-round. Gage is fairly new, but he's done a good job with the taproom and made a lot of friends. We look out for each other."

"I get it." Scott appreciated Liam's effort but wished he could nurse his hurt feelings on his own.

"I'm not from here, either," Liam volunteered. "I met my husband, Russ, when my car broke down. He's a mechanic. Luckiest breakdown I ever had." When Scott didn't say anything, Liam went on. "Which I'm telling you because we aren't against having new people here. The folks who are meant to be here find their niche. And those of us who stay watch out for one another."

"I'm not a threat," Scott replied. "I'm doing my best to protect everyone, especially the ones with abilities. The bad guys I'm chasing aren't anyone's friend."

"I know that," Liam said. "And I understand why you didn't

tell everyone the full story up front. But Gage really liked the person he met, and I think now he's wondering how much of that was real and how much was your cover."

"All of it was real." Scott didn't see a need to keep secrets. If he had ruined his chances with Gage, at least Liam could make sure Gage knew the truth. "I'm probably bad at my job falling for someone while I'm on assignment. And now he thinks it was some sort of James Bond thing to get information. I promise you —I'm not that smooth."

"Did you talk to him?"

Gage didn't usually confide in anyone about his love life, and he had barely met Liam. But he sensed that the librarian felt responsible for contributing to the rift between Gage and Scott and wanted to help.

"He's hurt and angry. We were supposed to go to dinner tonight but he begged off for time to think, which is why I'm here. I told him the whole story, but it might be too little, too late. So I guess I focus on my job." Scott couldn't help feeling a little sorry for himself.

"Give him time to cool down," Liam said. "For what it's worth, I didn't realize I was blowing your secret. Since you two were already cozy, I thought he knew."

"It just never seemed to be the right time," Scott said.

"No one in Fox Hollow wants the troublemakers you're hunting. With the psychics in town, it's a pretty good bet that the bad guys aren't any of our regulars. It's probably not proper procedure, but maybe we can help you catch them. After all, it's safer for our town if they stay far away from here," Liam offered.

"Thanks. I've probably made a mess of things with Gage, but maybe I can still finish my mission. I want to work things out with him, but if I can't, I'll go back to Albany and pick up the pieces."

Liam patted him on the back. "Don't give up on Gage so fast. He's hella stubborn, which goes with his other half, but he's also super loyal. If you both want to work things out, I have no doubt that you can do it." He glanced at Scott's drink.

"Do you need a ride back to where you're staying?"

Scott considered for a moment, then shook his head. "Thanks, but I think I need the walk. I parked out front, but I'll come back for it in the morning. Maybe if I get some sleep things will look better."

Liam looked like he wanted to argue, then shared a sad smile. "Okay. Call if you need anything. One thing I've learned about living in a town full of psychics is that if something is meant to be, it happens. Don't give up too soon."

Scott lingered a while longer after Liam left, nursing his drink. The music soothed his soul, and while he appreciated Liam's efforts to smooth things over, Scott wasn't sure it would be that easy to fix his budding relationship with Gage.

Maybe it's time I focus on doing the job. Gage will either forgive me or he won't.

He left a good tip and headed back to his motel. The wind had picked up, and Scott hunched his shoulders against it, flipping the collar of his jacket. He stayed alert, remembering the tough guy he had seen in the bar.

The foul garbage taste he had gotten in the bar from the stranger carried on the wind, alerting him to trouble. Scott felt certain the man had been up to no good, but that didn't mean he was a coyote.

Still, he felt watched. He kept an eye out for any animals who might be townspeople, but nothing stirred. That didn't rule out creatures in the bushes or trees, and Scott wondered how long it took to get used to having to wonder if every creature was really wild or a neighbor out for a stroll.

If I don't patch things up with Gage, I guess I'll never find out.

That thought left him sad as he made his way back to the motel, but he didn't dare get lost in his worries. Scott kept one hand on a taser in his jacket pocket. He had the guns SPAM had issued him but left those locked in his SUV, uncomfortable taking them on a date. He realized he might have misjudged how far it was to the motel as the walk took a while.

Who did I think I was fooling? I'm not cut out for this.

The garbage taste was stronger, and Scott heard a man's voice coming from a small stand of trees. "Yeah, I'll get the package from Paul Smith and take it from there. Don't worry—everything's fine."

Scott hung back, not wanting to be noticed. After a few moments, a car pulled up and the tough got into it and drove away. Scott made sure to get the license plate.

His motel room seemed empty and too quiet when he finally got back. Nothing had been disturbed, and none of his cameras showed any intruders. Scott spread out the maps. Paul Smiths was a small college town, not a person, and its location on Route 30 put it in a direct line through thinly inhabited territory that ran all the way to the Canadian border.

Maybe it's a handoff spot. Someone brings the drugs over the border and meets a contact to pass the package along. It could even be one of several spots, like the town of Malone that's a little farther north. Change the coyote and throw the cops off the trail. I need to work the case and do my job. I can't control what happens with Gage, no matter how much I want that to work out.

SPAM's computer systems were disturbingly thorough. Scott could log in from anywhere and access nearly all the features, which helped with research, especially when the information wasn't available through regular public sources.

He ran the license plate and found it registered to an eighty-year-old man in Tupper Lake, a town about halfway between Fox Hollow and Paul Smiths. That didn't help him identify the tough guy, but it did support his suspicion that the drugs were traveling down Route 30 from Canada.

On a hunch, he did a search on the man whose car had been used. According to the SPAM database, the old guy had a long list of priors, did some jail time, and associated with known supernatural syndicate members.

Scott didn't think the old man was likely to still be a crime kingpin, although stranger things had happened. But it did suggest that his house could be a likely drop for shipments, maybe even a lab for products requiring minimal equipment.

On a hunch, Scott did a search for abandoned places in the Adirondacks. The results came back with a variety of answers, but one stood out—an old Wild West theme park called Frontier-World. The park closed decades ago, but photos showed that many of the buildings were still standing.

It would be the perfect hideout, Scott thought. *No one goes there anymore; it's not near anything, and the coyotes could come and go without being seen. The town of Paul Smiths is closer to the border, and the old park is an hour farther south. Maybe the coyotes dump some of their cargo of finished drugs at Paul Smiths and use the old man's house in Tupper Lake as another drop. The old park would be perfect for a lab to combine the raw materials and make more.*

He noted his suspicions in his online logbook along with what he knew about the small town and the old man's house, and decided that a road trip would clear his mind.

Someone else can check into Paul Smiths and the house in Tupper Lake. I'm going to have a look at that theme park.

To his surprise, he received a reply quickly.

Surveil and report—do not try to intercept or handle this on your own. Send photos and details confirming location involvement, and we will dispatch a team.

Scott let out a relieved breath. His orientation had been skimpy, and it certainly didn't make him a seasoned agent with ninja moves after a few sessions. While he had always had a talent for finding out gossip, and his role as a journalist took advantage of those skills, his prowess with hand-to-hand combat was limited to the orientation at SPAM and the Judo classes he had taken in middle school.

Now that he had a plan, Scott felt better. He packed up his

materials and got ready for bed, lingering in the shower to wash away the day.

His thoughts ran to how he had hoped the evening would go before everything with Gage fell apart.

First, we'd go to that little Italian restaurant in the next town that Gage said he wanted to take me to. If it was candlelit and romantic, we would have bumped knees under the table and held hands, flirting up a storm.

Good wine, hearty food, and dessert—maybe sharing something decadent like cheesecake. We'd talk through dinner and the drive and get to know each other better.

I don't know his favorite movies or bands. Did he play sports in school? Do drama? Does he like to read? There's so much to find out.

His soapy hand fell to his cock, stroking himself as he envisioned the date that didn't happen.

We'd have joked around during dinner, found things in common, and shared bites of food. Back to Gage's cabin for a nightcap because I wouldn't have to drive home until morning.

We'd have a drink or two and turn on a movie, and make out for a while on the couch. Take it slow, both of us hot and hard knowing we wanted to go farther than blow jobs this time.

Before we got naked, we'd move to the bedroom. We could take each other apart slowly. I want to lick him all over, continue to find out what really gets him hot. There wouldn't be a hurry; we'd have all night.

Maybe we'd have started kissing, done sixty-nine, to take the edge off for both of us. Scott envisioned the scene like a movie, with his imagination filling in the blanks. Picturing them sucking each other off nearly made him come right then, but he gripped the base of his cock to stave off his orgasm a little longer.

After that, we'd need to work up to round two. Plenty of time for kissing and touching. We hadn't gotten to anal, but maybe we'd have gone for it tonight. Would he want it slow or hard and fast? Maybe something in between to make it last.

He fucked into the channel of his hand achingly hard. *I wonder which of us would top first? I'm fine with either—does he switch? I wouldn't mind bottoming for him—his cock would feel real good. But I'd love to see him come apart under me, get all sweaty and breathless, and lose control.*

Scott knew it wouldn't take more to push him over the edge. Picturing Gage in the throes of climax, lips pink, eyes half-open, gasping his pleasure, was enough to make him lose it. He came, spurting against the shower tile, reaching out with his other hand to steady himself when his knees went weak.

The build-up had been great, but the afterglow was non-existent. The hot water had grown cool, and when Scott opened his eyes, he wasn't pillowed beside a lover who might be his mate. Instead, he was alone, jerking off in a motel shower.

He sighed, feeling lonelier than before as he toweled off and pulled out a sleep tee and sweatpants. The temperature outside must have fallen because the heat had kicked on, filling the room with dry air and a musty smell.

Instead of crawling into a bed with nice linens in Gage's cozy cabin next to a very sexy man, Scott slid between scratchy motel sheets that smelled of bleach and fake flowers. The pillow was hard, and worst of all, he was alone.

Maybe tomorrow, things will seem better. Right now, I'm seriously thinking that SPAM picked the wrong guy. I don't know who I'm fooling. I'll do the best I can and try not to get killed, then I'll quit playing James Bond and go find a real job.

They say you should never meet your heroes. I don't know about that, but so far, living my childhood dream of being a caped crusader isn't working out so great either.

Scott ate breakfast at the Fox Hollow Diner. A tall man stopped at his table. "Are you Scott?" When Scott nodded, the other man smiled. "I'm Brandon. Liam sent me. Is it okay if I sit down?"

Scott shrugged, still nursing his disappointment. "Sure. Suit yourself."

Brandon slid into the bench across from him. "Liam told me about what you do." He held up a hand to forestall protest. "I promise I won't tell people. But I think I might be able to help."

He dropped his voice. "My other half is a moose. You saw Gage and me in the woods at the fire tower that day. And I've gotten to know some of the moose shifters in the area. We roam quite far when we're in our fur. I can introduce you to a Canadian Mountie who is also a moose shifter. They handle all kinds of problems. He might have heard something valuable—and he's doubly likely to be concerned since it's not only cross-border smuggling, but it's also shifter-related."

"Thank you. I'd appreciate the connection," Scott told him. "I'm not out to make trouble for people who aren't trying to cause problems. The folks I'm after pose a danger to your *community* as much as they do to everyone else." He hoped his stress on the word got his message across.

"Chad—the Mountie—is a good guy. He's got the whole incorruptible Dudley Do-Right thing going, except he's much smarter than the cartoon character."

"I hope so." Scott smiled.

"If you tell him the kinds of tip-offs you're looking for, he may have seen something that will help. And if he hasn't seen it yet, he'll know to keep his eyes open."

Scott tried to remember the glimpse he had gotten of his companion's moose. Brandon was tall and broad-shouldered, his dark hair streaked with lighter brown hues. When they finished eating and paid the check, Scott and Brandon left the diner and walked along the docks near the lake. Brandon called his friend and smiled when the call connected.

"Hey, Chad. I've got someone I think you need to talk to. He knows about us, and he's with US supernatural law enforcement trying to bust some bad guys who are messing about with stuff they shouldn't be," Brandon replied. "You will? Awesome." Brandon's smile broadened. "He's right here. Let me give you my phone." He handed off his phone to Scott.

"Hi. Chad. I'm Scott. I'm following up on tips we've had about coyotes bringing shifter-specialized drugs across the border. Illegal recreational drugs and medications that haven't undergone the usual testing or review. There have been deaths. We want to stop the smugglers and find ways to create useful medications and substances through legal channels."

Chad was quiet long enough that Scott thought the call had dropped. "I've heard about that but haven't run into it myself. It's a tough call. There's no quality control for the illegal medications, but they're filling a need that the legit producers haven't matched. And the people who need the meds are stuck in the middle. Either they don't treat their condition and suffer, or they break the law getting what they need wherever they can find it."

"I sympathize. I really do," Scott said. "But I think the paranormal community deserves safe pharmaceuticals. It doesn't do any good to treat a condition with medications that are useless—or worse."

"I don't promise to have the information you need, but I'll do my best to answer your questions," Chad replied. "Shoot."

"Did anything you hear have particulars about specific towns where the distribution is happening?" Scott asked.

Chad paused, and Scott wondered if his contact was weighing his words. "If you've looked at a map, you know that there are more trees than people around here—more so the farther you go to the north."

"I've noticed. It's beautiful here."

"We think so," Chad replied. "Of course when something goes wrong, it also means that there aren't a lot of witnesses or security cameras. If someone knows the lay of the land, they can cross the border in the forest and get pretty far before they come in contact with enough people to notice."

"That makes it tough. We can't watch every road, and the smugglers certainly know the area best. I'm guessing there are plenty of dirt roads that aren't even on the map," Scott replied.

"You would be right about that. And if the couriers are

shifters, they don't need roads until they're ready to meet up with their buyers," Chad replied. "When you said coyote was that—"

"Literal and slang," Scott said. "Our reports say that coyote shifters are carrying the contraband and handing it off on this side of the border. We can't really call the normal law enforcement partners in on that. If we told them we were arresting coyotes, they'd laugh us out of town."

"Probably so," Chad agreed. "But I can ask around and see what I hear."

"That would be a big help." Scott felt a jolt of relief. "If our reports are wrong, I'd be thrilled. But we've had enough input, I think there's something to it. And it's definitely something that should be left to law enforcement, because smugglers get dangerous when someone gets between them and their cargo."

"Yeah, I can see that." Chad paused. "When you're talking about altered substances, how far does that go?" A new wariness had crept in, and Scott wondered if his contact had made the possible connection to Gage's shifter-optimized brewery.

"I'm not worried about shifters who want to get buzzed or have medicines that actually work for them," Scott clarified, wishing he had done that up front with Gage. "I have leeway to turn a blind eye, and I intend to do that for mixtures that aren't hurting anyone. I don't want to stop people who need treatment from getting concoctions that help, even if they haven't gone through all the normal channels.

"But I don't have any patience for people who take advantage of folks who are vulnerable, and foisting fake drugs off on sick people is just plain evil, in my book." Scott took a deep breath, realizing he had gotten heated. "Sorry. I'm just a little passionate on this stuff," he added, feeling chagrined.

Chad chuckled. "That's okay. You've got a tough job. Good to believe in what you do." He paused for a moment. "You know I'm a Mountie?"

"Yes. And I'm with a government agency you've never heard of that focuses on paranormal problems," Scott replied.

"I *should* probably run this through channels, but I owe Brandon too many favors to count," Chad said. "Now realize that what I've heard could be urban legend. I don't have evidence, and I don't know anyone with first-hand knowledge. It's a whole lot of hearsay."

"That's better than a whole lot of nothing," Scott told him. "I'm all ears."

Chad laughed. "No, that's me. Have you ever seen moose ears?" He grew serious. "I've heard bits and pieces, nothing actionable, but some of it is probably true. The main labs are in Montreal and Ottawa, near the border. They brew up small batches that are optimized for fast metabolisms. Probably have buyers already lined up."

"The problem being, that there aren't legal alternatives for the medications," Scott commiserated.

"Right. Which makes this, to me, an ethical dilemma," Chad said. "On the monster meth stuff, yeah—it's poison and needs to get shut down. But if I had a condition that drugs made for regular humans didn't touch—or if I loved someone who did— and it was a life or death situation, and there were alternatives out there that were the only option…I can't say that I'd do the right thing," he admitted. "God help me, but it's the truth. So I have really mixed feelings about this."

"Yeah, me too," Scott said. "More since I've started looking into it. The bad actors need to be shut down—no question. But I'm not going to prioritize going after the people creating legitimately altered medications that help people with extra capabilities. I imagine I'll have a big list of projects when I get back. It could take me a very long time to work my way down." *Assuming I even stay with SPAM. Which I probably won't.*

"And the same goes for things like souped-up shifter beer. I'm a believer in equal opportunity when it comes to getting a buzz."

Chad let out a long breath. "Bless you. Not everyone would understand."

"Yeah, well. I can't promise my bosses would, so don't spread it around," Scott replied.

Chad paused. "Something else that might just be rumor, but I'll mention it. The *main* labs are in Montreal and Ottawa, but they say there are smaller labs scattered around to assemble the ingredients that come in from across the border. We shut those down as soon as we find them, but it's like playing whack-a-mole."

"Thanks," Scott said. "That might come in handy."

"Stay in touch, and don't take crazy chances," Chad warned. "If you need something, Brandon knows how to get ahold of me."

Scott handed the phone back to Brandon. "Thanks. That helped a lot."

Brandon looked at him skeptically. "You heard what he said. Those are dangerous people. Be careful."

"I will." Scott gave a wry smile. "After all, I'm a highly trained secret agent."

THE NEXT DAY, Scott picked up supplies at a convenience store before heading north to test his theories and got his guns out of the lockbox in the back of the SUV. He had slept restlessly, dreaming about Gage. In some dreams they were hiking, and in others they canoed or walked through a mall, but in each one Gage was far enough away from him to be out of reach.

He woke feeling out of sorts with a lingering sadness that he couldn't shake and didn't know whether it reflected his own insecurities or was a portent of an inevitable future.

Maybe I misread the psychic signals, he thought as he got ready for the day. *If we're really mates, we'd understand each other better. I guess I was wrong about that. I'm new at this. I seem to have made a mess of it, and we'd barely gotten started.* Those thoughts made him very sad.

His attempt to call in with a status report and ask April for insight into the case had not been successful.

"Thank you for calling SPAM," the automated system answered, even though he called on what they had told him was the special secret number just for agents. "All of our representatives are currently busy with highly classified, very important work. Please leave a message, and someone will get back to you.

"In case of impending alien invasion, please press one. If you are calling to report a zombie attack, please press two. For spectral activity, wraiths, and vengeful spirits, please press three. To report vampires and necromancers, please press four. To report evil warlocks or dark superheroes, press five. If you are a SPAM agent calling from the field, please press six."

Scott pressed six and waited, expecting to get a real person.

"Hi! I'm AImee, the SPAM AI Chat Bot. How can I help?" a far-too-perky automated voice replied.

"This is Agent Scott Dixon, calling in with a field report. I need to speak to April. It's urgent."

"All lines for that person are busy. We can't connect your call right now," the chipper computerized voice replied. "In a few words, please tell me what you are calling about."

"I'm closing in on the drug smuggling coyotes and request backup for a confrontation," Scott replied, chafing at the gatekeeping AI.

"For animal control, please hang up the line and call—"

"*Shifter* coyote smugglers, not animals," Scott said, trying to keep his patience.

"Please report border and customs issues to—"

"This is Agent Scott Dixon, and I'm calling to request backup," Scott repeated.

"Sorry, if you have an IT issue and need help backing up your computer, please call—"

"Not *computer* backup. I need people with guns to provide in-person support for invading the bad guys' lair."

"According to SPAM best practices, agents anticipating a physical confrontation should request support by giving twenty-four-hour notice and submitting Form 22-B—"

"I didn't know I was going to be confronting them," Scott argued. "It's not like I made an appointment."

"There's no need to get huffy," the AI said primly. "If you can't be civil, I'll be forced to end the call."

Scott took a deep breath. "I'm going to confront a bunch of smugglers. I would like to request armed physical support."

"I have emailed Form 22-B to you. Please fill it out in its entirety, and your request will be submitted for review. Please allow forty-eight-hour turnaround on any non-emergency requests," the AI responded.

"I'm trying to tell you—this *is* an emergency, and I need backup dispatched from Albany *now*."

"You don't have a right to talk to me like that just because I'm a disembodied intellectual asset simulation," the voice sulked. "I have feelings."

"Please put me through to a real person. Any person," Scott begged.

"I'm real. We are having a real conversation. My name is AImee. I exist."

Scott took several deep breaths. "Nice to meet you AImee. I need to talk with someone who knows about my case. Can you please transfer me?"

"I have accessed your case files and scanned them. I now know all about your assignment. I am equipped to be of help."

"I need physical support—people with weapons—to come to my location and help me invade the smugglers' lair," Scott replied. "It's not something that can be done virtually."

"That statement is hurtful to the unbodied, Scott. Please refer to the agent manual about the use of respectful language."

Scott closed his eyes and rubbed his temple. "Can I leave a voice message for April? Please?"

"I will put you through to April's voicemail. Don't think I won't report your disrespectful attitude just because you said please," AImee said. "Have a good day."

Scott heard a click, and then "Hi, this is April. Please leave a message at the beep. If this is an actual emergency, please return to the menu and ask AImee for immediate assistance."

Beep.

"April—it's Scott Dixon. I'm requesting backup to check the addresses in Tupper Lake and Paul Smiths, New York, that I put in my online log book. They're likely drops for smuggled drugs. I've got a lead that the coyotes are holed up in the old Frontier-World Park and might have a lab there. I'm going to go scout the area, and I tried to request backup but—"

"I'm sorry, but this mailbox cannot accept a longer message. Please email or call again later. Goodbye."

A dial tone rang in Scott's ear, and he stared at his phone incredulously.

That's just fucking fantastic.

Both his love life and his new job seemed destined to failure.

If I don't quit SPAM, I wonder if I could ask for a desk job. I could do a much better job answering phones. I don't think I'm cut out for this secret agent stuff.

Scott made up his mind that when he got back from exploring, he would try to make things right with Gage. *I think we had a spark. I'd like to see if we can put all our cards on the table and start over. If it doesn't work, at least I tried.*

He cranked up the radio and sang along at the top of his lungs, deciding that if nothing else, he would enjoy the road trip no matter how things worked out.

Hours later, Scott had seen plenty of the Adirondacks countryside, checked out the two locations, and had no new concrete leads.

Paul Smiths was a lovely mountain college town that boasted

good restaurants and plenty of activities for people who loved the outdoors. Like Fox Hollow, it was an unlikely crossroads for illegal drugs. The coyotes in their bad-boy leathers would have stuck out amid the mix of REI preppy and legit LL Bean students and adventurers.

The ruffians would be equally out of place in Tupper Lake, a charming hamlet full of outdoor activities, museums, live music, shopping, good food, and a beach. Scott found the house where the old man used to live. It had been purchased and renovated and was occupied by a family with children and dogs, hardly a ramshackle drug den.

He guessed that there could be abandoned barns deep in the woods outside those towns that could work for the smugglers' purposes, and maybe drones would find them now that SPAM had a heads-up of where to look, but he was unlikely to stumble upon them.

Looks like I've struck out at everything, Scott thought. He bought a large coffee and a cookie and found a bench where he could sit and look out over the lake before he drove back to Fox Hollow.

My big lead might have value, but not that I can validate right now. Maybe that's a good thing—I don't want to crash the smugglers' party and get killed. I'll make my report and see if SPAM can take it further.

And on the topic of crashing and burning…I've made a mess of things with Gage. James Bond never ran into problems because he had scriptwriters—and he wasn't real. Maybe I won't have to resign from SPAM. My first case will be such a colossal failure that they'll just fire me.

He checked the time and weighed whether to try to check out FrontierWorld, but it was an hour's drive in the opposite direction from Fox Hollow. By the time he could get there it would be late in the day, cutting into his time to explore before he lost the light.

If things are over with Gage, I've got no reason to hang around Fox Hollow tomorrow. I could head over to the old park early in the day and have plenty of time to have a look around. Beats sitting around feeling sorry for myself.

Scott decided to treat himself to a good dinner but didn't want to eat in Fox Hollow. He found an Italian place that rated well and indulged in pasta with an awesome house-made marinara sauce. Before driving back, he stopped at a liquor store and picked up a bottle of vodka for the room.

Shaken, not stirred. Very Bond.

He checked his phone for messages. No one from SPAM had responded. Gage had left several messages, but Scott was afraid to listen to them. He had carved out a fragile peace with his drive and planned to hang onto it at least until he got back to the motel room and had to confront the reality of his failure.

In the meantime, I've got Shrödinger's boyfriend—that place between being together and breaking up. Worrying about getting dumped isn't quite as bad as knowing for sure. Next time, I'll go the radical honesty route. Warts and all. Oversharing, TMI. And it will probably be the wrong strategy. But maybe it's right for the right guy.

I thought Gage was the right guy. But if this made him walk away, apparently not. Without Gage, moving to Fox Hollow is out. Maybe I'll find someone in Albany. I guess I could join an outdoors group. I might even learn to like it.

Scott tried to shake off feeling sorry for himself and mostly succeeded on the rest of the drive. He sang along to the radio and tried to appreciate the scenery. By the time he got back to his motel it was dark.

The big overhead neon sign cast the parking lot in colors and shadow. Scott glanced around and didn't see anyone. He had worn his Glock in a shoulder holster under a jacket all day, just in case he found the coyotes, but had taken the rig off while he drove and set it under his coat on the passenger seat. The shotgun was in the back.

I might need it at the old park tomorrow. I don't want a confrontation, but I hope I find something useful. It's bad enough to be unlucky at love, but at the moment, I suck at my job too.

Scott picked up the bundle of jacket and gun and tucked it under his left arm as he got out of the Pilot and locked it with a beep of the key fob. He pulled the door key from his pocket when he heard a scratching noise, and the taste of garbage and old cigarette ash bloomed in his mouth.

Coyotes.

Four forms sprang from the shadows. One knocked the holster and jacket out of Scott's hands, while two hit him full force at the knees, and a fourth jumped at his back. He staggered, reaching for his gun just as a man slipped from the darkness and swung at him, connecting with Scott's temple.

Scott felt blinding pain and knew he was falling, but he was unconscious before he hit the asphalt.

CHAPTER 7
GAGE

*W*hy are you angry at our mate? Gage's Mal demanded. *We just found him. Do you want to make him leave?*

He wasn't completely honest with us. He didn't tell the whole truth about who he was—or why he was here.

We haven't known him long. And we were busy with other things. Perhaps you should have sniffed his butt, his Mal suggested helpfully.

Sniffing wasn't exactly what had crossed Gage's mind in the dreams that woke him, lonely and hard. *Licking, fingering, and fucking sound like more fun.*

I liked him, his Mal sulked. *I don't want him to go away. He is mate.*

I need to be able to trust him, Gage argued.

He did not tell you everything all at once. How is that not trusting? Too much to tell, too little time. His dog consciousness was certainly persuasive, Gage had to admit.

He and Scott only had a few days together and a couple of dates. Gage certainly hadn't unloaded his whole sad backstory about family friction, ex-lovers, and all the reasons he ended up in Fox Hollow. Or mentioned that he was a shifter. Not that he didn't plan to share, but there hadn't been time.

And I'm not sworn to secrecy by the government.

Gage realized he had been staring at his computer screen for minutes without doing anything. He let out a long sigh and reached for his cold cup of coffee.

I overreacted.

You think? his Mal snarked back. *Bite first, ask questions later? If I'd have done that, I'd have gotten sent to a trainer.*

I'm not good at dating. Or letting down my guard. Or falling in love. Gage's track record for relationships was spotty at best. He had viewed dating as a distraction from his goal of creating new recipes and building the brewery. While that was all-consuming for a while, he kept himself too busy to realize how lonely it was despite evenings spent surrounded by people.

Guess I'm not as over Kris as I thought. Gage had dated Kris in college and thought they had something special, although he had never been tempted to disclose his shifter side.

Still, they seemed like a good pair, and Gage enjoyed Kris's company. Until he found out that Kris had been dating him to get close to one of his friends. That blew up spectacularly, splitting their friend group and leaving hurt feelings all around. Gage lost both Kris and his friend, their gang was never the same afterward, and Gage ended up feeling like the bad guy because he called Kris out on not being truthful.

Kris is not Scott's problem. Never blame the grass when the garden hose sprays you.

Is that some weird Malinois secret wisdom?

He could have sworn his dog snickered. *It's still true.*

Gage sat on the stool in his brewery's kitchen where he prepared the mixtures that went in the vats to make the beer.

I don't know what to do. I was really hurt because Scott told others something personal before he told me. I overreacted. Liam thinks I'm an idiot. Scott probably never wants to see me again. The thought of not reconciling with Scott made his heart hurt.

Mates, remember? Trust that. And go scoop your own poop, as we say, his Mal said.

I made the mess; I need to clean it up.

Before he worked up the nerve to call Scott, Gage scrolled through several message boards for craft brewers. He wondered if there was a similar non-supernatural effort to what SPAM was doing to find unscrupulous brewers adulterating their batches with questionable or illegal additives.

Gage hoped not. Craft beer was a relatively recent passion for him, but he had fallen in love with the whole process. He loved working with brew masters to design a new taste profile, watching over the batch as it matured, and holding his breath as tasters got to sample. When it was good, Gage felt euphoric. And when it was bad…a whole vat could go down the drain.

I made a fool of myself. Now I've got to eat crow.

Crow? I don't think that would taste good, his Mal objected.

Not real crow.

How do we eat it if it isn't real? His Mal wanted to know.

It's a saying, like your bits of wisdom about poop. It means to swallow your pride and admit that you were wrong. Which tastes bad. Like crow. Or poop.

*Actually—*his Mal started to object.

Yuck. I don't want to know. TMI, dude.

Do I make fun of you when you eat fish? his Mal said.

Actually, yes.

Gage figured there wasn't going to be a better time to swallow his pride and dialed Scott's number. When Scott didn't pick up, Gage wasn't sure what to do. He didn't want to go too long without trying to fix things between them, but it wasn't the sort of thing he liked leaving on voicemail.

"Hey, it's Gage. I'm sorry. Please call me. I overreacted, and I want to fix things. I care about you." He wasn't sure what else to say, so he ended the call.

Once you fix things, will there be licking and humping? his Mal asked, sounding a little too curious.

Don't be vulgar. But yes, with luck. I hope so.

Will we be happy? I don't feel good in my middle.

Gage frowned, worried. *Are we sick?*

My heart hurts, and my stomach makes me think we should go eat grass.

Gage gave a sad chuckle. *That's the downside of being in love. When it's good, you feel like you've had too much really strong beer. And when it hits a snag, you feel like you drank too much cheap beer, and you want to puke.*

It had been a long time since Gage had been in a relationship. *Maybe too long. I've forgotten how it works.*

He didn't really believe that, but he was willing to admit that his people skills were rusty on the dating side. Getting along with total strangers in the taproom was one thing. Being vulnerable and admitting that he wasn't self-sufficient took skills he hadn't used in a long time.

Maybe I can make a peace offering. I'm connected to a lot of other small-batch and craft brewers in private groups online. I could ask questions to see if they've heard about people trying weird additives. They wouldn't know it was for shifters and supernaturals, but there might be rumors.

Gage logged in to one of the more active groups and did a quick search to make sure no one else had already broached the subject. Nothing seemed to have been posted, so he took the leap.

I'm hearing rumors of brewers experimenting with enhanced formulations to appeal to patrons with higher-than-average metabolisms. Has anyone had luck with that?

Gage figured the post was normal enough not to raise eyebrows but tapped into the essence of what the rogue beermakers were doing. It could take hours to get responses, depending on who was online, so he skimmed a few other chat threads since he hadn't been in the group in a while.

A side thread about additives ranged from flavorings to sweeteners to instructions for making weed-infused brew. He skimmed over those but didn't see anything unusual or supernatural about the posts.

He switched over to a server that was only for users with paranormal abilities. The moderators were cyber-witches who could verify users' claims and ruthlessly bounced pretenders. That kept it safe for conversations that didn't need to reach the mundanes.

Gage posted the same question and hit enter. Figuring it would take a while to get responses, he checked his email, signed off on invoices, and was just about to listen to voicemail before his computer pinged.

The people doing the experimenting are a pretty closed group and a rough crowd, one response read. *Might be good to keep your distance.*

People used pseudonyms on the server, so Gage doubted he could find out real names without major hacking. The response intrigued him, and he wondered if the rough crowd were normal competitors or more like the troublemakers focused on a supernatural clientele.

Cut-throat competitors? he asked, purposely misunderstanding.

The reply came back quickly. *That's one way to put it. Just trust me, you won't want to mess with these folks.*

Gage tried to come at the subject from a couple of directions, asking about ingredients and brewing methods. No one seemed inclined to provide details, but the posts all warned him away from asking questions.

That response didn't give him details, but it supported Scott's warning that the people involved were more dangerous than the usual highly competitive beer fans.

Then Gage spotted a sub-chat marked special cases. Curious, he clicked on the link.

"This discussion group is for brewers and beer lovers whose physical conditions require specialized formulation," the description said. "You will be required to disclose your condition in order to join."

Since Gage had created a profile under a false name, he played along. "Shifter," he typed in the corresponding box.

That won him a password. "Pay dirt," he said. He made a note of it before clicking and scrolling down the topics.

"Best beer additives for shifters over fifty pounds. Beer additives to avoid for vampires. Natural ingredients that react badly with magical abilities," he murmured as he scanned the topics.

Anyone outside the community might take the list as a joke or the overdramatic styling of goths, but the details struck Gage as authentic.

He skimmed the topics without commenting, trying to remain as relatively anonymous as possible until he knew what —and who—he was dealing with. The last thing he needed was trouble following him back to the taproom.

Another half hour made it clear that he wasn't the only one brewing for shifter metabolisms and that there seemed to be some degree of disagreement over which additives or ingredients were permissible and which were not. Fortunately, since Gage preferred an all-natural approach, nothing he had used in his first batches ran afoul of the consensus of allowable mixtures.

Now and then, he picked up a veiled warning in the comments about being careful of buying from unfamiliar suppliers, or using ingredients from unproven sources. The writers didn't come right out and say that doing so had consequences for magical and psychic talents, but anyone aware of such things would get the message.

Buried deep in the threads was a discussion of which additives might spell trouble with law enforcement or the conventions of different supernatural groups. Some of the concerns focused on whether the enhanced brews could cause a person with special abilities to lose control or impair their judgment to the degree that they posed a threat to others.

While that wasn't different from the danger of overconsumption for people without magic, not knowing one's limit for a witch or a vampire could have more dire outcomes than getting in a fender-bender or stumbling down the steps.

Reading between the lines, the biggest warning lay in reminding readers with special abilities that they remained safer by not doing anything to confirm their existence. While a pack of drunk wolf shifters might howl at the moon, a gang of blitzed vampires could lay waste to an entire hamlet and out the magical community to their mundane neighbors.

All of which were concerns Gage had considered before opening the taproom. He had long conversations with his neighbors in the Fox Hollow community on the pros and cons, and while everyone acknowledged the potential downside, support for the taproom had been overwhelming.

We've lived among mundanes for thousands of years, one person responded to the survey. *They tell tales about the ones who weren't good keeping secrets, but in all those years, no one has proven our existence because a were or vamp got shit-faced and ate a town.*

Gage thought back about incidents that history blamed on bad grain or fermentation gone awry. Now, he wondered whether the problems enshrined in those accounts had more to do with someone meddling with the recipe than a weakness of the audience.

His mind wandered, and he checked his phone, hoping for a message from Scott. The sharpness of his disappointment only served to reinforce his and Mal's conviction that he and Scott were mates and meant to be.

Is he safe? He's in Fox Hollow to poke around and ask the hard questions. Did he ask the wrong people and get found out? And if he disappears, who do I notify?

Gage had no idea how to get in touch with Scott's people at SPAM and wasn't sure he wanted to attract their notice.

Instead, he focused his attention on organizing paranormal participant tasting panels for his new brew, Moonlit Nights. Two panels with different people, covering a wide variety of supernatural abilities, animal types, and body sizes would give him a good idea of the potency of the new beer and its appeal.

Once the panels were scheduled, Gage moved on to the request from the Fox Hollow Hotel to do a special tasting event. They could run it with open sign-up and crosscheck later to see who had abilities and who didn't. That way, Gage could get feedback from mundane drinkers as well as his true target audience. Ideally, people without paranormal talents could still enjoy the beers without any ill effects, like any normal brew, and those with abilities could feel relaxed and buzzed.

Would Scott come? Have I ruined everything?

If they really were fated mates, it should take more than a minor tiff to seriously damage their relationship. But their pairing was so new and felt so fragile that Gage couldn't help worrying.

Once he finished the day's paperwork and emails, he checked his phone again, hoping for a response. He had a signal, but Scott hadn't replied.

Gage didn't know whether to be hurt, pissed off, or worried. He knew that the most likely reason Scott wasn't picking up on the call was work-related.

He came here to do a job, not look for love. He's still got bad guys to bust, even if we're at odds. So he's probably just working, looking for those bootleggers. Maybe he wouldn't have asked for my help even if we hadn't argued, but I'd feel better if we were together. I might be able to protect him.

We could sniff them out, his Mal offered. *We have a much better nose. And shifters have a different scent. We could be of service.*

Gage had noticed a long time ago that shifters and weres of an animal smelled different than the normal creature itself. A shifter wolf, a werewolf, and a wolf-wolf had subtle variations in their scent that he could pick up in his animal form but which didn't register when he was human.

I don't know how much help he's allowed to ask for on secret government stuff, Gage said. *That's the whole secret part.*

Silly not to ask. We know the woods. And we could keep him safe.

Gage agreed with his Mal, but he didn't know that Scott would see things the same way. Most of all, he worried about Scott poking around looking for information on the smugglers who clearly didn't want to be found.

He wasn't expecting a repeat of Prohibition-era machine guns and bootlegger brawls, but then again, maybe that wasn't so far-fetched if the coyotes had money on the line. They weren't likely to roll over quietly and let the feds shut them down. Gage wondered why Scott had been sent in alone, without a team.

Maybe the idea was that he would get the lay of the land and report back, and a team would show up. Of course by then, if the bad guys caught on, they could be long gone.

If Scott's intel was correct, the bootleggers posed a threat to the entire supernatural community. Unsafe products under-mined trust, and bad mixes meant people could get hurt. Since potency was at the heart of the issue, reformulations done without concern for safety could leave customers sick or worse. Untried additives could trigger allergies or make it difficult for customers to respect their limits.

It was a bad business all the way around, and Gage knew he should be glad that the powers that be were looking into it to protect them, but part of him worried about outsiders learning more about their community. He wasn't including Scott in that description, but it definitely extended to his bosses and the brass in Washington, DC.

Gage checked his email and phone messages one more time, then decided that he needed a break. His landscaper friend had told him that the next property was already marked for holes whenever Gage had time to dig, and Gage thought that sounded like the perfect thing to take his mind off Scott, smugglers, and bad beer.

He turned up the radio on the drive over, doing his best to keep from dwelling on his worries. When Gage reached the new location, a large lawn in back of a rental home, he shifted in the car and bounded toward the stakes that marked where new trees would be planted.

The cool air perked him up, and the breeze ruffled his fur. Gage's Mal ran zoomies around the perimeter a few times to stretch, getting lost in the sheer joy of movement. His large, muscular body was built for speed, and when he really got going, he had all four paws off the ground between strides.

Ears twitching, tongue lolling, Gage gave himself over to his Mal, pushing worries aside. Once he had run off some anxiety, Gage trotted back to the water dish his client provided that automatically filled so he could refresh himself between digs.

He felt better already and eyed the first spot where a hole was needed. Dirt flew as he sank his claws into the moist ground, sending soil flying. His big paws didn't take long to make a difference. Gage opened up a shallow hole of the size indicated by the stakes, then dove in to make it deep enough for planting. He didn't stop until just his head remained above ground when he sat inside.

Half a dozen spots were marked, but Gage knew the landscaper's timeline and realized that he didn't have to dig them all today. He satisfied himself by digging a second pit, then trotted to where a hose had been rigged up so he could stay in his dog form and still turn the water on and off to clean up. That avoided neighbors seeing a naked man frolicking with the garden sprayer and calling the cops.

Once was embarrassing enough.

Gage shook off. It didn't take much with his short, slick coat. He stretched to his full length and arched his back, feeling the burn. Gage threw his head back and took in a deep breath, then froze.

Coyote.

He had only run into the scavengers a few times while he was in his fur. The average coyote was a bit shorter and weighed less than the average Belgian Malinois, and Gage was on the taller and stockier end of the spectrum for his breed.

That was an advantage one-on-one, but coyotes ran in packs. While Gage felt confident he could hold his own against one of the scavengers, he wouldn't want to try his luck against a group.

Sometimes a coyote is just a coyote, Gage thought, realizing that merely picking up the scent didn't mean these were smugglers Scott was after. He had heard that some of the animals in the Adirondacks were coyote-wolf hybrids while others had domesticated dog ancestry.

Gage caught the scent again, stronger now. He had no desire to have a confrontation, but it intrigued him to find the coyotes relatively close to town. Gage knew that the crafty predators were famous for their adaptability and often coexisted with humans in towns and cities. But this felt less like sharing territory and more like an incursion.

Curious, he followed the scent. Gage didn't spend much time prowling, well aware that strangers might see his guard dog as a threat, shoot first, and ask questions later. He had roamed this section of woods often and not encountered coyotes, so he was intrigued whether their presence now was coincidental or had something to do with Scott's investigation.

I'll just check it out, and if there's something suspicious, I'll report it to Scott when we talk again. I won't try to do anything on my own.

As he slipped closer, he heard human voices.

"Need to change our route. Let things cool down," one man said.

"Fuck that. Everything else is cross-country or out of our way. The more round trips, the more money," a second man countered.

"What are they going to do? Try to trap us? We can get out of those," a third person argued.

"Yeah, but hunting and trapping is legal here," the first man pointed out. "We get shot in our fur, we're still shot."

"Don't get shot," the third man replied.

"I told Big John that we needed to switch things up, not have a routine," the second speaker said. "The money's good, but I've got no intention of ending up in jail—or Animal Control."

"You're overreacting. No one is paying any attention." The first man sounded confident. Gage wondered if he was one of the bosses or just a courier.

"There's a fed sniffing around," the second speaker said. "That's bad news."

"Nothing we can't handle," speaker three said. "People have all sorts of tragic accidents up here in the big woods." Their chuckles raised Gage's hackles.

He didn't like the odds of three to one, and Gage had no way of knowing whether more of their pack lurked under the trees. Gage knew he couldn't stick around in case the wind changed and they caught his scent. While he was confident about his fighting skills—having learned the hard way in tussles with his four military brothers—Gage knew the best fight was the one avoided.

Save it for backing up Scott. It sounds like we can help, Gage thought.

His Malinois instantly bristled. *No one hurts our mate.*

Gage made it back to the car without pursuit. He climbed inside before he shifted, then locked the doors and dressed.

Do I tell the sheriff? I don't want to compromise Scott's investigation. I trust Sheriff Armel, and Scott did brief him. Gage felt a twinge of guilt about his jealousy. *I was thinking like a boyfriend. Scott was thinking like an agent. I owe him an apology.*

Gage checked his rearview mirror frequently on the drive back, but since he had left the woods before the coyotes, he didn't think they could have beaten him to the road. Whether or not they sensed his presence and alerted a comrade by phone, he didn't know, so he stayed wary.

When he reached Fox Hollow, he let out a breath of relief. He decided to go to Scott's motel and beg forgiveness, patching up their relationship and assuring himself that Scott was okay. Gage had no trouble following Scott's scent to the right room, but his SUV was gone, and no one answered when he knocked.

Standing outside the unit, Gage tried to reach him again, but the call went to voicemail. "Scott—please pick up. I'm worried. I'm sorry I was an asshole. I'll make it up to you. I want to work this out. And I've got a lead, I think, on your case. Please—call."

He checked his messages just in case but found nothing. *Dammit, Scott! Check your phone.*

Please be okay. I need to apologize and move on to hot makeup sex.

Gage drove straight to the police station. He asked for the sheriff at the front desk, and a few minutes later, Armel bustled out.

"What's up, Gage?" Armel greeted him. "Need a permit for a kegger?"

Gage managed a weak smile in response. "Nothing quite that fun. Can we talk in your office? This is me doing the see something/say something drill."

Armel quickly sobered. "Sure. Right this way." He glanced at the officer at the desk. "Hold my calls."

Armel ushered Gage into his office and shut the door before moving around his massive desk to the tall chair behind it. Gage took a seat in front.

"There's a pack of coyotes behind the golf course plotting trouble." He explained how he happened to be in the vicinity.

"You heard them yourself?" Armel prodded.

Gage nodded, still debating how to handle the rest of it. He decided that honesty was his best choice, even if some of his knowledge was hearsay.

"I know about Scott being a federal agent and that he's here looking for bootleggers," Gage blurted. "These guys in the woods—they knew the feds were onto them, and they plan to get rid of him if he gets in their way."

"Whoa. Slow your roll. Back up and explain," Armel said. "You were out there, why?"

Gage explained about the hole digging, expecting a smart remark from the sheriff.

"Glad you found a way to work off that big Mal energy without digging a trench through town," Armel said. "I'll mention you to the Parks and Rec manager. You could end up with an excavation business on the side."

"Anyhow, I caught the coyotes' scent and went to see what was going on. They were in human form—still stank." He recounted what he had overheard. Armel's smile faded, then disappeared altogether, turning to a worried frown.

"You're sure?"

Gage cocked his head and gave him a look that was pure Malinois.

"Okay, okay. Don't bite. Had to ask," Armel held up a hand in appeasement. "Shit. I don't like that at all. Have you heard from Scott?"

Gage squirmed in his chair. "No. I tried to call, but it went to voicemail. We had a tiff—"

Armel cocked an eyebrow. "Tiff? Something I ought to know?"

Gage looked away. "We really hit it off, and then we had an argument. It wasn't such a big deal that he wouldn't return my call, so now I'm worried."

Armel sniffed the air, and Gage belatedly recalled that bears had the best sense of smell of any animal. "Mates?"

"We're still working that out," Gage replied. "But yes."

"Lord love a duck," Armel muttered under his breath. "Spare me the lovers' quarrel."

"It's not like that," Gage said, although it really was. "He wasn't sure he could trust me because I make paranormally enhanced beer—although mine is all natural and locally—legally—sourced. Liam found out about him being a spy and mentioned it, but Scott hadn't told me, even after we...never mind.

"Anyhow, I'm worried. Even if Scott is totally okay, we've got bad guys smuggling stuff near town, and someone's going to get hurt sooner or later—tourists or locals. Not counting the dangerous cargo. And I don't want anyone else thinking my beer is contraband."

Armel raised an eyebrow. "I am aware of the situation," he said in a wry tone.

Gage tried to ignore that Scott had confided in yet another person, even if it made perfect sense. "Yeah. Of course. The coyotes have a very distinctive odor even when they're in human form. Smells a lot like trash."

"Well, that fits," Armel grumbled. "Did you get a look at the men in the forest?"

"Just a glimpse. They looked like every bad stereotype of biker toughs—leathers, scruffy, pretty rough. They'd definitely stand out if they came into town like that," Gage said.

Plenty of motorcycle groups came through the Adirondacks in the summer, and almost none caused trouble as far as Gage heard. Armel had a reputation as a no-nonsense sheriff who didn't put up with problems, and Fox Hollow's tight community could close ranks to protect the residents. Troublemakers went elsewhere.

Armel ran a hand back through his thick brown hair. "Shit. We've got lots of campers in the woods and tourists in the area. We do *not* need a Capone-level shootout."

Gage's heart fell at the thought. He didn't want Scott or any of his friends getting hurt in the crossfire.

"The rest of my family is military," Gage told the sheriff. "Special forces, police, search and rescue. My dad was a bomb squad veteran who raised us more like cadets, assuming we'd all follow in his pawprints. They did—I wanted to brew beer.

"But I know how to track and fight. And if they have my mate, I need to be part of the plan, or I'll insert myself anyhow," he said, part volunteering and part warning.

Armel muttered something under his breath Gage didn't catch, and he figured it was just as well.

"You're saying I should put you in protective custody—"

"No! I'm saying I want in on the action if Scott needs rescuing. And if you need backup running those coyotes so far out of town they can't find their way back."

Armel chuckled. "Don't get your hackles raised. I get it. Good to know I couldn't keep you out of it if I tried. I worked with a Malinois once. He made the German shepherds look like sheep. Toughest cop I ever knew. Other than one Yorkie shifter who was positively psycho."

He held out his hand, and Gage saw the faint white scars of two small incisors. "See this? That damn Yorkie thought I was reaching for his lunch."

"He bit a bear?"

"He would have bitten Godzilla if it came between him and his food. Like I said—psycho."

Gage thanked the sheriff and promised to let him know if he heard from Scott.

Are you just going to leave it like that? Our mate is missing, his Mal demanded.

Hell, no. But I've got to figure out how to look for him without interfering with a federal investigation—or making things worse. I don't want to blow his cover.

You don't want to blow his cover, just him, his Mal added with a snicker.

Not the right time. We need to make sure he's safe, help him catch the bad guys, and then we can get our sexy on.

Gage drove to the library, feeling twitchy. He couldn't go back to the taproom and focus on doing paperwork, and his head bartender was in charge of setting up tonight's event, so Gage would just be in the way.

He checked—once more—that all the shipments had come in and been put away, and that no one had called out. That meant he technically didn't have anything urgent to do until the night's event at the taproom.

Gage tried calling Scott again, with no luck and no answer to his email or text. He forced himself to think.

Am I being ghosted?

He never wanted to be one of those guys who couldn't take a hint. But the vibes he had gotten from Scott were full speed ahead, the sex had been hot, and other than the tiff over Scott not confiding in him, nothing else had gone wrong. Scott had seemed honestly excited about getting together again and taking their relationship further.

And there's no denying the definite mate connection. I should be able to trust that above everything else and to know if he was lying. Withholding information isn't being completely truthful, but it's not exactly a lie. Maybe I'd suck at being a secret agent's partner. It would take some getting used to.

Gage thought about that for a moment. He had let Scott's job title slide off him like it was emergency room physician or firefighter—demanding jobs with long hours and danger. But the people in first responder roles weren't spies. They didn't have to infiltrate enemy organizations under false identities or be sent undercover into life-or-death situations.

I don't honestly know if I can do that. I think we could be great together, and I'm already falling in love with him, but would the life break us up?

Gage had grown up around military families, and he knew that sometimes the stress, relocations, danger, and secrecy took its toll on marriages. That was one reason he didn't want to follow his family tradition. He valued the sacrifice and commitment, but he wanted to brew beer that made people happy and let them forget their troubles.

Does that mean we're doomed from the start? I don't want to make him choose between me and his job, and I don't think I'd be happy leaving Fox Hollow at this point. I've never heard of SPAM. Maybe it doesn't work like the CIA or FBI. Maybe he doesn't have to go away for long periods of time. After all, Fox Hollow isn't far from Albany. And there are other, very normal, jobs that require travel. The choices are pretty limited here in Fox Hollow. It wouldn't be fair to say he has to relocate or only do a job that is needed here.

But I don't want to leave the taproom. Sure, I could start over somewhere else, but my community is here in Fox Hollow. I love what I've built. Can we make this work?

The questions made Gage's heart hurt. His Mal whined and nudged his mind, offering solidarity and comfort.

He is mate. We will figure it out, his Mal insisted.

Gage didn't know of anyone who had found their fated mate and didn't stay together unless one of them died. Even then, mates rarely outlived each other by long.

I hope so. I already feel too much for him for this not to be fated. We're still getting to know each other and yet I feel like he's always been a part of me.

That means it's real, his shifter side replied.

CHAPTER 8
GAGE

Gage walked into the library and felt calmer just from the smell of books and the familiar sight of the shelves and couches. He had loved going to the library ever since he was a kid, where the quiet atmosphere made him feel secure, and the limitless knowledge gave him big dreams.

The library was one of his safe places when his brothers got too rowdy or their teasing was too intense. Gage could slip away and lose himself in adventures or discover new facts about one of his many hobbies. Whenever he felt at a loss, the library offered sanctuary, community, and answers.

He was hoping it wouldn't fail him now.

"Hi," Gage said to the person at the front desk. "Is Liam in? I'm Gage. He's expecting me."

She pressed a button and looked up with a smile. "I've let him know. You can wander around or find a seat. He'll be with you shortly."

Gage took the opportunity to wander. He checked out the community art display with recent works by local residents of all ages. The new books table caught his eye and he made note of several titles that he wanted to add to his reading list. The aquarium, with its brightly colored fish, was a favorite stop. He watched them swim and wondered if fish shifters were a thing. That brought him to the terrarium with its mini ecosystem like a private world.

"I wondered where you wandered off to." Liam came up behind him. "Enjoying the view?"

"Just impressed by how much goes on here," Gage replied. "You do a fantastic job of community engagement."

"Pfft. It's not just me. Our whole staff pitches in with ideas and connections and time organizing and moderating. But I am inordinately proud of what goes on here in any given month." Liam preened. Gage thought the gesture definitely resembled Liam's fox side.

"I'm looking forward to your Library Nights," Gage told him.

Liam had proposed doing a series of evening programs linking books about brewing to tastings at the taproom. Gage had been surprised to find out how many thrillers, cozy mysteries, fantasy novels, and romances used breweries and distilleries as major elements in their plot.

That led to the idea to do book and beer pairing events where people were encouraged to read and discuss the featured alcohol-related book at the taproom with drink specials and snacks. Gage's bartenders had enjoyed trying to come up with unique cocktails tied to the stories. Everyone had a good time, and the events were some of the taproom's most profitable evenings.

Given Liam's out-sized personality, it always amazed Gage that the lively fox shifter had chosen a profession that fostered a reserved atmosphere.

Then again, he's the Pied Piper to the whole community, matching us with thrilling adventures.

"Is this still a good time to plan the next couple of events?" Gage asked.

"Sure. Let me make sure we don't get disturbed."

Liam spoke quietly to the volunteer at the front desk and gestured for Gage to follow him into his office. The snug space had floor-to-ceiling shelves filled with books, a large collection of fox figurines, and a framed portrait of a very handsome wolf whom Gage recognized as Liam's mate, Russ.

"This is perfect. And before we start, have you heard from Scott? He asked me to look some information up for him, but I haven't been able to get him to answer his phone," Liam asked.

Gage's instincts went on high alert. "You haven't? He hasn't answered me, but I thought he was just annoyed at me. I checked his motel yesterday, but he wasn't there."

"You guys had a lover's spat." Liam made it a statement, not a question.

Gage knew Liam's interest was sincere, even though the fox never liked to be out of the loop on local news.

"I overreacted when I found out about him being a fed and that he had told other people about his reason for coming to town but not me since we had started to get close. We argued. I called to apologize, but he didn't pick up. I've left messages, and he hasn't called me back," Gage admitted. Liam was a true friend, and Gage respected the solid relationship Liam and Russ had put together.

Liam offered Gage coffee from the single-brew maker on the windowsill. Gage accepted it gratefully.

"I'm sorry—I thought you already knew," Liam said. "It's not that unusual to have bumps at the beginning. There's so much to learn about each other and so many old triggers. It gets better."

"I hope he'll give me another chance." Gage hadn't intended to come here and spill his guts, but he was doing exactly that.

"Are you kidding? I was barely around the two of you, and I can see that you're mates. I spoke to him after. He hasn't given up on you yet. Let him cool off, and you can make it up to him," Liam replied with a salacious wiggle of eyebrows.

"That's the problem—he's not answering his phone, and he isn't at his motel. I'm worried," Gage said. "I know he's here to do a job, but he shouldn't try to tackle those coyotes alone."

Liam frowned. "You think that's what he did? Did you talk to the sheriff?"

"Yes to both. Armel doesn't know where Scott's gone, either. I'm not happy that SPAM sent him here without backup," Gage admitted.

"Yeah, it's a big forest for one agent. And coyotes—real and metaphorical—tend to operate in groups," Liam agreed. "He didn't tell me anything about his job. But I may have done some snooping. I didn't find much, just that they recruit people with minor special abilities to work for the greater good," Liam continued. "I don't know what his talent is, but Dr. Jeffries probably does. And I'm very sorry that I caused friction between the two of you."

Gage sighed. "That's on me being an asshole who is out of practice being in a relationship. I got butthurt about not being in the know, but I guess if I started out as a possible suspect, he wouldn't blow his cover by telling me."

Liam shrugged. "I could point you to the whole poetry section on how love and logic don't always go together. Come to think of it, that's half of literature too. So you're not the first."

"I guess it's supposed to be comforting that the idiot table is crowded?"

"You can take anything you want from that," Liam said with a laugh. "Did you have some new ideas about Library Nights?"

"Actually, I did," Gage said and launched into the possibilities he had compiled. It felt good to set his worry for Scott aside since he saw no way to help or change the situation at the moment.

Liam had a list of his own, and some of their ideas spilled into possibilities for related craft evenings where taproom patrons, for a small fee, could work on an art project that they took home with them after an evening at the bar and a couple of drinks.

"I was thinking that over the summer, we could do something with wilderness adventure books," Liam suggested. "You know, like having an actual wilderness guide comment on Jack London's books or Whitman's time in the forest."

"That sounds really good," Gage said. "People read those, come up here, and think that's what they're going to find—"

"And have to get rescued by the rangers," Liam finished with a sigh. "Yeah. Happens every year. At least shifters don't get lost."

"I bet we could get Madden and Elias in on this with comics," Gage added. His squirrel-shifter friend Madden and Madden's partner Elias ran the local comic shop and were very popular with Fox Hollow residents.

"We could even do a movie night with a forest-themed film and discussion over themed brews." Liam flushed with excitement that brought a glow to his cheeks and emphasized his red hair. "Like watch one of those monster-in-the-woods-killing-campers horror flicks and talk about all the things they did wrong."

"That would be fun around Halloween," Gage agreed. He had opened the taproom more than a year ago and had been so focused on running the operations smoothly and creating a core set of proprietary brews that he had let the marketing be largely word-of-mouth.

On one hand, that kept the taproom from getting overwhelmed before it was able to provide the best experience. At the same time, Gage almost had to take out a loan when finances were thin. Now that they had found their footing and a loyal clientele, he wanted to attract seasonal traffic, tourists, and people who might come more for the event theme than the actual beer.

"So, now that we have that figured out—how are we going to help Scott find the bad brewers?" Liam asked with a conspiratorial grin.

"Isn't that interfering in a federal investigation? It's not going to help our relationship if I get sent to prison."

Liam sat back in his chair and laced his fingers behind his

head, looking every bit the wily fox. "First, they have to catch you. Second, if there are criminals running illegal substances near Fox Hollow, I'd say that the residents have a stake in the game."

"I'm convinced." Gage grinned. "But there's a whole lot of nothin' between here and the border in terms of forest without roads or towns. People carrying contraband would need to stick to roads or trails. But if they're using coyote shifters, they can cut cross-country, and the area is so vast that there's no way to find them, even with satellite photos."

"Let's see if Madden can stop by." Liam grabbed his phone to text their friend. "He needs to be in on this."

Ten minutes later, Madden showed up, practically vibrating with energy, as always. Gage marveled at how Liam and Madden somehow managed to channel their shifter sides into their human personalities. Liam was sly and witty. Madden's rampant enthusiasm was nearly its own type of superpower.

Then again, I've been told I give off bodyguard vibes even when I'm human, Gage thought.

When it's true, it's true. We can be one scary SOB when we try, his Mal agreed.

"Oh, we're doing an investigation? Count me in. You want to know what's going on in the woods? Ask a squirrel," Madden said enthusiastically. "We are *networked*. We joke about it being the 'inter*nut*,' but that's not far off. The only ones who know more are the birds. Sometimes we can get them to join in for a good cause."

Gage and Liam exchanged a look. "Really? That might solve a couple of problems." Gage caught Madden up to speed and swore him to secrecy. That was probably a lost cause, but since Scott had confided in a couple of people to get their take on the situation, Gage hoped he would be forgiven for bringing Madden in on the problem.

"If we help him take down a notorious drug gang, do you think they'll do a cable documentary?" Madden asked.

"That would expose the shifter community and blow Scott's cover," Gage pointed out.

"Right. Bad idea. But I had to ask." When Madden got enthusiastic, he spoke really fast and practically vibrated in his seat. That was one of the most fun things about including him in their RPG Night—he got very into the adventure.

"Tell us more about the internut," Liam said.

Madden's eyes shone bright. "So it's like that old game of telephone, only with squirrels. There are thousands of us out there, different species, but we all speak the same chatter. I tell ten squirrels what I'm looking for, and they each tell ten, on and on, until someone finds the answer. Then the info goes back up the chain until it gets to me. Best of all, it's fun—and no one expects squirrel spies."

"Wasn't there an old cartoon about a squirrel spy? I thought I saw it in reruns when I was a kid," Liam asked.

"Yeah. Secret Squirrel was awesome," Madden said with a swoon. "My dad got really mad when I cut eye holes out of his hat so I could dress up like the character for Halloween."

Gage was only partly listening. "That could be a fantastic way to help—and since no one ever looks up, the coyotes aren't likely to realize they've been surveilled. The squirrels can look for Scott at the same time to make sure he's okay."

"Okay—fill me in. I need to know what to tell everyone to look for," Madden said. "It's gotta be easy to explain and remember, or we'll get a flood of tips and never be able to sort through them."

Gage thought for a moment. "On the drug side, we're looking for coyote-shifters making a regular trek from the Canadian border into drop locations in the Adirondacks and back again. Could be solo, might be small groups. The shifters are likely to be outlaw types when they're in human form. They would be moving packages, delivering them from the border, going back for more. They may leave the bundle for someone else to find or meet a contact and hand it off."

Madden frowned. "Yeah, none of that would be normal. What do you want the network to do?"

"Leave them alone, observe and make notes, and report back," Gage said. "They definitely should *not* try to get involved. They'll be a huge help just by alerting us to the locations of the drug drops and the paths the coyotes are taking."

He paused. "Here's the more urgent thing—I think Scott may have gone out to find them on his own. So they're looking for a blond man with curly hair who could be lost, hurt, or even being kept prisoner. Maybe being held in a remote cabin or an abandoned building. I don't think they would move Scott too far outside Fox Hollow if that makes it easier."

"And if they find him?" Madden looked dangerously excited about the whole search-and-rescue operation.

"Tell them not to get involved unless Scott is in immediate danger," Gage said. "We don't want them getting hurt. If they can chew through rope, great. If not, stay back and wait for a chance to help us get to him or for him to get away."

"Got it," Madden replied. "I'll see if we can get the birds in on it too. We could cover a wider territory. Don't worry, Gage. We'll find him and bring him home safe."

Gage appreciated his friend's confidence and was grateful for his help. His first priority was rescuing Scott. Stopping the smugglers was a distant second, although if they could provide a break in the case—once Scott was safe—it would be good for SPAM and the community.

He hadn't heard of a problem with drug use in Fox Hollow, but then again, most of the residents wouldn't have the same reactions as regular humans so the cargo would be largely wasted. Perhaps it was possible that some of the tourists and campers were really picking up drug drops, but if so, they had been good enough not to arouse the suspicion of the sheriff or the rangers.

Gage remembered the coyotes he had spotted in the woods and the conversation he had overheard about switching routes.

As pretty as the Adirondacks were, the huge forest was sparsely populated, and large areas weren't easily accessible by road. Plenty of lakes made seaplanes a good option for some routes, and Gage wondered if any of the pilots were part of the illegal drug and pharmaceutical syndicate.

Every time I try to narrow the scope, I come upon something that makes it even bigger.

Gage scrolled through his contacts and called Jeffries, who picked up on the second ring.

"Gage—I was just about to call you," Jeffries said. "Where is Scott?"

"I don't know—which is why I decided to call," Gage said. "I'm afraid he's in trouble."

Jeffries was quiet for a moment. "Damn. That's what I wanted to tell you—I had a vision about Scott. Just a glimpse, but I think you're right."

"What did you see?" Gage held his breath.

"It was jumbled and dark, but it looked like he got jumped by several men. There was a fight. He was outnumbered. They knocked him out and took him away."

Gage swore under his breath. "Damn. I was afraid of that. I don't want to compromise his investigation, but I'm doubting he was able to let SPAM know. So a search party isn't likely, and they won't be on the way to rescue him. I think he needs our help."

"I agree," Jeffries said. "We can pull a group together and keep the knowledge to a fairly small cluster. Let me make some calls. Can we meet at the taproom at noon?"

"Absolutely," Gage said. "I've already spoken to Liam and Madden. They're making plans as well."

"I'm sure they are." Jeffries chuckled despite the seriousness of the situation. "They'll be good for recon. I can bring a couple of psychics in on that piece as well. We need a witch on our side since we don't know what the other side has. And if we're going to go after him, we'll want the Lowe brothers and Brandon, plus the sheriff. That's not a big group, but it packs a punch, and it gives us some varied abilities."

Gage's head spun, realizing they were planning to go to war. "Okay," he said, glad to be taking action. *Maybe all that training when I was growing up will be useful, after all.*

"If we're lucky, they won't realize he's a fed and figure him for a nosy cop," Jeffries said. "He's got value as a hostage. They might be willing to change their routes away from this area altogether if it's too much trouble."

"You seem to know a lot about this sort of thing." Gage was a little weirded out by how easily Jeffries slipped into a tactical role.

"I've helped on some other dicey situations since I've been in Fox Hollow," Jeffries told him. "And back in Ithaca, the cops wouldn't admit to asking psychics for help. We had to promise to keep it hush-hush, but they brought us in more often than people suspected when law enforcement got stumped."

"I thought that stuff only happened on TV."

"Nope. It's more common than you'd think. The cops worry that they'll get made fun of by the press or that the city council will cut their budget for hiring us," Jeffries replied. "Then a psychic will help break open a cold case somewhere, and all of a sudden, the police departments each want their own."

"Thank you." Gage felt a spark of hope. "I didn't know what to do."

"That's one thing I love about Fox Hollow—we know how to take care of our folks. Go back to the taproom. I'll call you once I have more details."

Gage thanked him again and drove back to his bar. Just as he parked, his phone rang, and Gage was surprised to see it belonged to Sheriff Armel.

"I realized there's someone else you should talk to," the sheriff said. "He's fairly new in town—moved up from Albany not long ago. Austin Williams. Private investigator, ex-cop. He got involved looking into disappearances from an old mental institution that happened back in the day, and it ended up being linked to bad drugs and shifter trafficking. He might not know anything helpful—but then again, he might. I just texted you his number."

"Thank you," Gage said. "And I think something happened to Scott—Dr. Jeffries had a vision and Scott still isn't answering his phone."

"Hmm. I get why you're concerned," Armel said, "and you're right to say something. But he's a fed on a case. He might have gone dark for a lot of valid reasons. Maybe he didn't want the phone to tip anyone off he's watching a site. I'll have someone check the motel."

"I'd hope the motel would have reported gunshots or a fight," Gage said.

"I'd hope so, but it depends on the clerk on duty. Some of them just don't want to get involved unless there's no way around it," the sheriff said. "I'd warn you again about getting mixed up in his case, but if he has disappeared, we need something to go on to find him."

"Dr. Jeffries is pretty sure about his vision that something bad happened to Scott, so I think he really is in trouble."

"Damn," Armell muttered under his breath.

"Madden and Liam are handling surveillance. Dr. Jeffries is calling in a few friends to help once we get the intel to narrow down the territory. I'll call Williams and see if he's got any insights," Gage said.

"You don't waste time." Armell sounded impressed. "You've gone to the right people. My team here isn't intended for search and rescue or busting drug syndicates. But park rangers are officially law enforcement, and they take a dim view of shenanigans on their watch. I'll see what I can find out—and if I hear anything about Scott or find any clues at the motel, I'll let you know. Keep me posted."

Gage promised to do so and then dialed the number Armel had given him.

"Williams Investigations. Austin Williams, speaking," a man's voice answered the phone.

"Sheriff Armel gave me your number," Gage blurted. "I'm Gage Merrick. I run the Merrick Craft Brewing taproom. A friend is in trouble. Can we meet to talk?"

"Sure," Williams replied. "First half hour is free, after that, standard rates apply."

"Fair," Gage said. "Meet me at the taproom? How soon can you come?"

"Can you give me an idea—"

"I think a pack of shifter drug smugglers kidnapped a federal agent, and the sheriff said you'd run into people making altered medicines when you dealt with an old hospital," Gage replied.

Williams was quiet for a moment. "Okay. Wow. Yeah, all right. I can be at the taproom in ten. Blond guy, mid-thirties."

"I'll watch for you. Thanks." Gage ended the call, and only then realized he hadn't asked William's standard rate.

I can't shake the feeling that Scott is in big trouble. He's my mate, so I should be able to pick up more through our bond, even if it's new, but I'm not getting anything except static and vague worry.

Maybe I've made a mess of his investigation, and he'll be angry if he's gone undercover or off doing recon. We're new, he's doing a job, and he doesn't owe me a rundown of his schedule. But who else is going to notice that he's gone missing if he's really in trouble? I guess SPAM might if he never reports in to his superiors, but how long would that take? And would they send more strangers to look for him? If he's in danger, it'll be too late by then.

Gage knew he was probably rationalizing, but Armell didn't seem to think he was overthinking the situation.

He's our mate. Trust the bond, his Mal told him. *He needs us.*

The taproom was quiet this time of day. They weren't officially open yet, and while the kitchen crew was prepping for the day, the dining area and bar were empty.

Gage waited by the locked doors until a man he didn't recognize walked up and tapped on the glass. He fit the description Williams had given, and Gage let him in.

"Austin Williams." The man extended his hand.

"Gage Merrick," he replied, giving a firm shake. "Let's talk in my office. I appreciate you coming out on short notice."

"You gave me one hell of a pitch." Williams laughed. "I couldn't turn that down."

Gage offered Williams coffee and poured a cup for each of them from the pot that was always full behind the bar. They carried their drinks into Gage's cramped office, and Gage cleaned files off the guest chair.

"Sorry—things have been a little crazy," he said about the mess. "Please, have a seat."

Williams sipped the coffee and sat. He gave Gage a look like he was memorizing every detail and running it through a mental database.

"Something about smugglers, altered drugs, and a missing federal agent?" Williams nudged. "How about if you start over and give me the story and we'll figure out how to fill in the blanks?"

Gage started from the beginning, and Williams listened with intense focus. He interrupted a couple times for clarification, then let Gage pick up the story again.

"There's too much empty space between here and the border to search without more intel," Gage said as he wrapped up his story. "But if the coyotes have taken Scott, we need to find him."

Williams was quiet for a moment as if he was buying himself a moment to pull his thoughts together. "What did the sheriff tell you about my old case?" he asked.

"Nothing, really," Gage said.

"Okay." Williams stretched out his legs and crossed them at the ankle. "Havenwood Hospital was an old-school mental hospital back in the day. It closed down quite a while ago, and stories started to circulate. I got hired by an elderly woman who wanted to solve the mystery of what happened to her brother, who had been sent off in the 1960s."

Williams took another swig of his coffee, and his gaze grew distant. "A lot of the people locked up there were shifters or psychics. To control them, the docs kept the patients drugged to the gills. In the process, they formulated some special drugs that worked on supernatural metabolisms.

"Everything the hospital did was illegal, so the drug piece was just a part of the bigger problem. Jamie and I put together a fairly long list of patients who disappeared and looked into it. Many of them had died over the years."

"Jamie?"

"At the time, a researcher at the local historical association. Now, my husband," Williams replied. "Anyhow, we couldn't locate a few of the missing patients. We talked to psychics and got an earful from their ghosts. We discovered that when the hospital received a new patient with abilities, they sold them off to the highest bidder to someone who wanted a captive psychic." Williams's disgust was clear in his voice.

Gage's stomach churned. "Fuck. How long did that go on?"

Williams's expression grew angry. "Way too long. Needless to say, people didn't like us poking into the situation, digging up old dirt. They gave us enough grief that I realized that even though the hospital closed a long time ago, there were people out there running the same rackets today. We reported what we found to the FBSI and turned copies of the files over to them to handle it from there."

Gage knew the S stood for supernatural, one of several government law enforcement groups—like SPAM—that handled paranormal crimes without admitting the existence of such things to the general public.

"Do you think anyone from those days is still around?"

Williams drew a deep breath and let it out again. "Anything's possible, but I doubt it. They'd be pretty old. Since those days, both the government and private hunters have gotten a lot more involved policing crimes against people with abilities. I've heard plenty of opinions about how that's worked out, but it's not the wild, wild west like it used to be."

"The drug runners must have a contact," Gage said. "And since the couriers are shifters and the drugs are made for people with abilities, I'm thinking that contact isn't a regular human. Maybe a shifter or a vampire—or a witch."

"Did Scott have any intel on that piece?"

Gage shrugged. "Not that he told me. He was playing things pretty close to the vest, but he did talk to the sheriff and Dr. Jeffries, and so did I. Dr. Jeffries gave me your contact info." Gage ran a hand back through his hair. "I'm worried. It's been hours with no word from Scott."

Williams's eyes narrowed. "What's your connection? Why do you care so much?"

"Scott is my mate." Gage met the private investigator's eyes levelly, daring him to make a smart remark.

He was pleased when Williams didn't blink. "Good enough. I'm guessing your bond is fairly new?"

"Yeah. And I don't want to mess up his investigation, but both my mate bond and my spidey sense is telling me something's very wrong. And Dr. Jeffries had a vision."

"Spidey sense?"

"Intuition. I'm a shifter so that accounts for the mate bond. I got into craft brewing to formulate beer that shifters and people with paranormal metabolisms could get buzzed from. And that connection led Scott to check to make sure I wasn't one of the bad guys, using altered additives for more nefarious purposes."

Williams blinked a few times. "That's a lot to unpack."

"Do you think there's a witch involved?" Gage asked.

Williams frowned. "What makes you ask?"

"The whole issue Scott was investigating was tied back to unscrupulous magic. The coyotes are shifter couriers, but they aren't creating the drugs. I guess it could be a human who knows about pharmaceuticals and paranormal physiology,"

Gage said, "but it seems more likely to be that there's a witch in the mix somewhere."

"There's a guy named Jennings Weston who keeps popping up like a bad penny," Williams replied after a moment. "He apprenticed to a couple of powerful dark witches who have been taken care of by other hunters, over in Ohio and down in West Virginia. Weston got away, but he's powerful and ambitious, and now some of the elder witches who would have kept him in check have been killed."

"I haven't heard that name," Gage admitted.

"Don't go looking for him by yourself," Williams warned. "We have people with abilities here in town who can approach him if it comes to that." He drank more of his coffee, and Gage wondered if the PI was weighing how much to disclose.

"I won't," Gage said. "I've already talked to Dr. Jeffries and the sheriff about mounting a search. But my mate's in danger, and I don't trust the feds to care enough to save him."

"Fair enough," Williams agreed. "There's some history involved you need to know. It'll tie some of the loose ends together for you—and for Scott when we get him back."

Gage appreciated Williams's positive attitude. Deep inside, Gage felt nervous and terrified despite the plans put in motion.

"There are a couple of hunters who killed a very dark witch, and now they're going after his coven of disciples," Williams said. "They've tracked down and eliminated a handful, but there are more from the coven out there. Weston apprenticed to one of those witches, Willis Osborn, who created illegal drugs and unregulated pharmaceuticals for paranormals out in Cleveland.

"When Osborn died, the drugs moved through a cultish wellness center in West Virginia run by Fletcher Swain, another of the dark witch's disciples. After the hunters caught up with Swain, Weston came up here. No telling whether he had heard the stories about the doc at the old asylum, but those days were long gone," Williams said.

"Of course, supernatural creatures have long memories. He

could have found someone who knew details from the old days and started to cook up his own drugs," Williams added. "I haven't looked for him, and he hasn't come to light, but he'd be the logical suspect in my book."

"How do I find him?"

Williams stared at him. "Did you not hear a word I said about not going after the witches on your own?"

Gage shrugged. "Never said I'd go alone. Maybe Weston has nothing to do with Scott's disappearance. But I don't think the coyotes are cooking the drugs. They're runners, not chemists or head honchos. It would make sense to have a witch involved—and that means a loose end Scott might not have known about."

"How long has Scott been missing?" Williams asked.

"Since yesterday. He didn't say that he would be out of touch. The sheriff said his SUV was at the motel, but it wasn't there when I stopped by earlier in the day. So he didn't go anywhere unless he left with someone else. My connection with him—the mate bond—is staticky, not clear. What I'm picking up from him is jumbled. I'm worried that he's hurt or drugged."

"Do you have something that belongs to him or that he had in his possession recently?" Williams asked.

Gage reached into his pocket and pulled out the scrap of paper that Scott had written his phone number on. "Will this do?"

"Let's find out." Williams took the paper in his right hand, and laid his left hand over top of Scott's. He shut his eyes and slowed his breathing.

For a couple of minutes, nothing happened. Williams's face took on a look of intense concentration. Gage felt a tingle where their skin touched and a buzz in the back of his mind as if the contact activated something within him. The focus of his mate bond grew sharper, and in his mind, his Mal sat up, ears twitching, on high alert.

Gage saw Scott sitting in a wooden chair, tied with rope around his chest. His wrists and ankles were also bound. Scott's badly bruised face and black eye made Gage's heart ache, and his inner Malinois growled a warning.

Mate is hurt. His inner Mal sounded ready to attack.

We'll bring him back, Gage told his other side. *First, we have to find him.*

Find him soon, fix him, bite the ones who hurt him.

I totally agree, Gage said, feeling his shifter's anger surge through him.

Gage had watched enough TV shows to know he should concentrate on picking up as many clues as he could. He wondered how much additional detail Wilson took from the same vision.

Although the image wasn't completely clear translated secondhand from Williams, Gage looked around the room where Scott was imprisoned. It looked like the cabin with rough-hewn walls had an oddly Old West feel.

As quickly as it appeared, the vision faded.

"Did you see that?" Gage asked breathlessly.

Williams nodded. "Yeah. I did."

"What did the Old West have to do with anything?"

Williams smiled. "Everything—because it tells us where he is."

"I don't understand."

"There used to be a western theme park nearby called FrontierWorld," Williams said. "It opened in the 1950s when American families got cars and going on road trips was a big deal, and it petered out in the late 1990s because tastes changed and there were lawsuits over injuries."

"You think the coyotes have Scott there?"

Williams nodded. "It would be a perfect place to hide. It's less than an hour from Fox Hollow. There are buildings still standing from the old park, and no one goes there nowadays. I remember hearing people talk about it, although I never got to visit. It was done up like a western town from cowboy movies with a live rodeo, a saloon, and a gunfight on Main Street every day at noon. For the kids who grew up watching Davy Crockett and Daniel Boone on TV, it was a dream come true."

"I was more into spaceships than westerns," Gage admitted. "But if the old theme park is that close, they wouldn't have had to travel far with Scott. And if it's deserted but still has some buildings suitable by coyote standards, it would work to hide him and also store the drugs. No one would have any reason to go there."

Williams nodded. "If we're going to check out FrontierWorld, we should also look at Tahawus. It was a mining town that was deserted nearly overnight when the mine shut down. There are some buildings left, but no one lives there. Another place where drugs could be stored or cooked where people wouldn't notice."

"We need to do something," Gage urged. "Scott looked hurt. He needs our help."

Williams held up a hand. "Slow down. We've got to think this through. It doesn't do anything for Scott if we go in, guns blazing, and people get hurt, or the coyotes vanish to another location and take him with them."

Gage knew the ex-cop was right, but he hated the delay. "I really don't want to contact SPAM and tell them we misplaced Scott. They're too far away to help, and I'd like to avoid getting him in trouble."

"Agreed. And I don't think we need to," Williams said. "Our folks can check both sites out much easier than regular law enforcement. If we're wrong, it was a hike in the woods. But if we're right, and we assemble the right crowd, we can save Scott and stop the coyotes."

He gave a sly smile. "After all, I think wolves, a moose, a fox, a bear, and a Belgian Malinois could hold their own against a pack of coyotes."

CHAPTER 9
SCOTT

can't believe I let them get the jump on me. Scott's head pounded from getting punched hard enough to make his vision swim and black him out.

When he came around, he was hogtied and lying in the back of a panel van that stank of coyote. Every bump in the road jarred his teeth, and the ridged floor of the commercial van didn't blunt the impact.

The bitter, dirty taste in his mouth told him that coyotes were still nearby. Scott struggled to remember what happened because his head ached almost too hard for him to string thoughts together.

Scott had fought back but there were too many attackers, and after one blow made him see stars, he went down in a heap.

Then he had been in the van, and after a drive, he had been hauled out and dragged inside a building. He remembered feeling a jab and feeling strange before he blacked out again. Somewhat awake, Scott realized he had no idea where he was or how long he'd been out.

He heard voices, so he kept his eyes closed. Looking around could wait.

"What do we do with him?" a man said.

"Nothing. He's a fed, so we'll get rid of him when the time is right," a second man replied. "For now, he's bait. The spell and drugs should keep him out of it. He might have been stupid enough to work this job on his own, but if he has a team and they come for him, we can nab them too. Tie it all up with a bow."

Scott's heart beat faster, and he hoped the coyotes weren't paying attention or couldn't pick that up. Even though the shifters were in human form, Scott got a garbage taste in his mouth.

"You think anyone will come after him?" First Guy asked.

"Dunno—but if they do, we'll be ready for them. And once we get them out of the way, we'll have a clear path to move the goods from the border all the way to the big markets down-state," Second Guy replied.

Definitely drugs. We were right about their operation. Maybe they were expecting us all along.

"What about that shifter town? You think they're gonna cause problems?" First Guy asked.

"If they do, we'll handle them. What good is having a witch if he doesn't get to come out and play?" Second Guy replied in a tone that promised trouble. "Weston's got enough mojo, I think he can handle all the furries in Fox Hollow."

Shifters aren't furries, dumbass. Who's this Weston guy? A witch? Shit—that makes this mess even worse.

"Still don't know what we need the witch for," First Guy said. "He gets a cut and for what?"

Scott heard the smack of a slap and guessed the other guy backhanded his companion. "Watch your mouth. You never know who's listening. And Weston does plenty. He puts spells on us when we cross the border so we're hard to see, and he does things to make the cops get busy looking somewhere else. He keeps the shifters and the bloodsuckers in line."

"Yeah, but the weres and the vamps don't cross the border.

We take all the risk, and too many others get a cut of the profit," First Guy grumbled.

"You want to take that up with the boss? Be my guest. When you disappear, can I have your coat?"

"Go fuck yourself." The two wandered out of earshot, leaving Scott alone, and the taste in his mouth faded.

Shit. Getting away from a bunch of half-wit coyote runners is one thing. Giving a witch the slip is another.

When Scott looked around, he thought he was hallucinating. He found himself tied to a wooden chair in what could only be described as a Wild West saloon that had seen better days.

An ornate bar beckoned cowboys and dance hall girls to slake their thirst. He could easily picture liquor bottles on the empty shelves behind the bar and a man in a striped shirt with sleeve garters serving beer and whisky to parched cattlemen and fancy women.

Against another wall sat the ruins of an old player piano, missing a front panel and most of its yellowed keys. Broken tables and tangled chairs filled the middle section. Dust and mildew covered everything.

Was this a movie set? Maybe I'm hallucinating.

The room looked like the saloon in every western he had ever watched, ready for the black-clad villain or the hero in a white hat to stride in for their dramatic cue. A stage lined one end, its red velvet curtains hanging in tatters, fallen prey to mold and mice.

Many of the front windows were broken, and the others were too dirty to see through. Saplings and scrub plants had overgrown the front porch, scraping against the remaining glass. A large, circular iron chandelier hung overhead with cracked or missing globes covering the…light bulbs?

Definitely not authentic. Scott's head hurt, but he still had enough of his wits about him to process the anachronisms.

Now that he knew what to look for, he saw electrical sockets in the walls and speakers tucked discreetly into corners.

Not to mention that there probably weren't cowboys or cattle drives through the Adirondack mountains back in the day. Guess I found out that the coyotes really are holing up at FrontierWorld. Fuck.

Scott guessed it had been a couple of decades since the last piano player and gambler walked away, and the curtain fell on the final chorus line.

He had a vague memory of stopping at this sort of western-themed attraction as a very young child on a family road trip. Back then, seeing people in cowboy outfits riding horses, facing down bank robbers, and saving the town had been big stuff. He had gotten a sheriff's badge and a hat, which he had treasured.

Now that Scott thought about it, he hadn't seen an attraction like that for a very long time, at least on the East Coast. *Probably too tame for today's kids. But I sure thought it was fun back in the day. Then again, working for a secret government agency isn't everything it was cracked up to be, either. Now I'm living the secret agent gets captured and tied up by the bad guys part of the plot, and it's not fun at all.*

He tested the ropes that bound his chest to the back of the chair, tied wrists together behind him, and secured his ankles to the legs of the chair. The knots held, and the rough hemp dug into his skin. Scott figured from the sun shining outside that he had been gone longer than he first thought. It was dark when they'd caught him in the parking lot.

We postponed our dinner date, so Gage won't have a reason to look for me since he's still pissed.

He remembered the voicemails he had been too afraid to listen to and wondered if Gage really had intended to break things off or was open to giving him a chance to come clean and start over.

I'll never know if I don't make it out of here.

By the time he missed his check-in with SPAM, it would be another day and anything could happen.

Did it look like I was jumped? If there's no sign of struggle and no blood—and the door to my room didn't get kicked in—there's not much for Gage or the sheriff to go on if they do decide to look for me. They might suspect that the coyotes got me, and there might be security camera footage of me getting my ass handed to me by a bunch of toughs, but after that, I just vanish.

I can't die here. There's too much I haven't said to Gage, too many things we haven't done. I want to explore this new thing between us and fix it so we have a fresh start. If we're right, it's a mate bond, a forever pairing. I want that kind of connection with Gage.

No telling how long it will take for someone to figure out what happened. The coyotes are tough SOBs, but they're professional enough not to leave a lot of easy evidence. I guess I need to save myself instead of waiting to be rescued.

Scott scanned his surroundings with a critical eye. The bar was in poor condition, but not as bad as it would be if it dated from the 1800s. *I was probably right about the defunct theme park. It wasn't made to last if it's all set dressing. Nothing should be as solid as the real thing. I can use that. Plus it's all falling down, so as a prison goes, it sucks. I've got to get out of here.*

Scott tested his chair. It squeaked and gave a little under his weight. He looked around again, making sure no one was watching, and began to twist, rock, and hop the chair until the wood splintered.

Need to avoid getting a splinter in my ass. That would slow me down.

The old wood cracked and sent Scott tumbling onto the floor. He shifted to catch himself on his knees and shoulders. The broken chair loosened the ropes, and Scott wriggled free.

He looked around, hoping his struggle hadn't made enough noise to attract attention. When no one appeared, Scott took stock.

Dead leaves, cobwebs, and trash littered the saloon. Dented beer cans in one corner suggested trespassers had found the spot for a long-ago party. The building smelled of mildew and disuse, but Scott could glimpse what it might have looked like in its heyday beneath the faded paint and cracked glass.

He stood and stretched, stiff from not moving for several hours. The headache and grogginess made him think his captors hadn't been kidding about drugging him. He did a quick check and found his protective charms were gone.

Damn. I came looking for the coyotes moving the illegal supernatural drugs. Guess I found them.

Scott patted his pockets, unsurprised to find his wallet, phone, and taser also gone. *They looked at my ID, that's how they knew I'm a fed. At least they didn't kill me right away. Maybe they're waiting for orders? That might have saved my life, but someone will be back sooner or later.*

Scott prowled the barroom, looking for weapons. His missing items were nowhere in sight. He settled for one of the chair legs. It probably wouldn't survive more than one hit, but it was the closest thing at hand.

I wonder if the guys who grabbed me will think to turn off tracking. If not, SPAM might be able to find me—if they know to look. If Gage notices, the sheriff could probably request my location, but that won't happen fast.

I've got to get myself out of here.

Scott picked up a couple of pieces of rope and wrapped them around his waist to keep them in case they came in handy later. At one of the tables, he found evidence that his captors had recently been drinking and smoking. A half-used matchbook and partial pack of cigarettes went in his pocket, along with a bottle opener.

He stuck an empty beer bottle in his pocket. Scott didn't want to make noise by shattering the bottom to make a weapon. The mirror behind the bar had been smashed in one corner, and he added a shard of glass to his loot.

Anything can be a weapon. SPAM training hadn't gone heavy on hand-to-hand combat. The people in charge relied heavily—too heavily—on their superpowers even though those abilities were, by definition, minor. Now, Scott wished he had paid more attention to tactics in high school wrestling instead of how the tight uniforms fit his teammates' asses.

Wrestling didn't teach me much about fighting, but it played a major role in my sexual awakening.

Scott searched his memories for anything useful he had learned from shows, comic books, or movies, since SPAM training had been big on enthusiasm and light on practical tips.

If the amusement park has been left to rot, it must not be close to town or the land would be too valuable. So once I find my way out, I'll have a hike.

Unlike in more populated places, Scott couldn't count on finding a gas station or restaurant every few miles. He could hitchhike, but that might lead to a whole different set of dangers.

His head hurt, making him wonder if he had a minor concussion. He had a fizzy lime aftertaste in his mouth, something he had learned to associate with magic. *Could mean there's a witch nearby, or that I got whammied when they knocked me out. Or both.*

He still felt hungover, making him more certain he had been drugged.

They didn't kill me outright. Why? They said I was bait. Maybe they have more confidence in the feds rescuing me than I do. That's a good thing, but getting me out of the way would have been simpler for them. So what's the advantage?

Did they know I was a SPAM agent before they kidnapped me, or did they think I was just regular DEA or law enforcement poking around?

Thanks to government turf wars, the creation of the DESA—S for supernatural—lagged behind other organizations like the FBSI. That contributed to the mess Scott had been sent to help clean up—unregulated prescription and recreational drugs sold through illegal channels.

While the bigwigs argued over whether a supernatural DEA would lead to exposure of the paranormal community and experimentation, opportunists took advantage of the gap between supply and demand. The need for drugs optimized for faster metabolisms was real and wasn't going to go away. Dithering just fed the problem Scott had been brought in to fix.

I'm definitely going to have opinions about what to do differently if I ever get out of this. And if I can get Gage to forgive me, and he wants to take this thing between us further, I'm all for it. Life is too short to miss out on the good stuff. First, I have to survive.

Armed with his makeshift weapons, Scott ventured out the back door of the saloon. He could make out where paths and fences had once wound through the woods, although the paths were nearly lost to overgrowth, and the fences had rotted.

He figured he was on the back side of the attraction's main street. From this angle, he could see the outline of the fancy signs that camouflaged mundane buildings to fit the theme.

Scott had a death grip on the chair leg as he slipped between the buildings to the front and got his first look at what remained of FrontierWorld.

A short length of asphalt ran between storefronts made to look like the Old West. Although the paint was peeling and faded, he could read the signs Mercantile, Chuck Wagon, and Arcade, giving him an idea of what the street must have looked like in its heyday.

Scott found a sign with a map and stopped to get his bearings. FrontierWorld's downtown was his current location and led to the main gates. He had no idea how many coyotes were in the pack, or whether they had other places to be, but until they realized he had broken loose, he had a grace period to escape.

Fanning out around the shops were other areas—Haunted Mine, Country Fair, Sweetgrass Village, and Rodeo Farm. Scott figured they would have been fun back in the day, but now all he wanted was to escape and find his way back to Fox Hollow.

Scott made his way toward the main entrance, sticking close to the buildings. The attraction must have been well-built to have survived decades of decay and not have crumbled by now.

When the main entrance sign came into view, Scott's heart

sank. A chain link fence surrounded the defunct attraction, and two armed guards patrolled the gate.

Shit. Scott figured the park had to have a back way in for deliveries and employees. He backtracked, hoping to avoid notice.

The road took him to an area with large barns, overgrown pastures, broken wooden fences, and an arena with grandstands that were collapsing in on themselves. The faded signs promised cowboys with lassos, trick riding, and bull roping. Even in decay, Scott could almost hear the cheers of the spectators and wondered how many theme parks were haunted.

Probably more than I want to know.

A cluster of clapboard houses around a small park looked like an idyllic pioneer village. More signs announced shops for yarn, pottery, toys and fudge and a grandma's kitchen snack bar. A gazebo in the park looked like the perfect spot for live music or craft demonstrations.

Back in its heyday, the fake small town had probably been charming. Now, the darkened windows and damaged roofs looked post-apocalyptic.

Scott didn't know when he might run into a patrol or the coyotes might catch his scent. He hurried on, crossing under a red-white-and-blue sign proclaiming the next area to be the county fair.

Once upon a time, the fair probably held a dozen classic rides like a Ferris Wheel, Tilt-a-Whirl, and Scrambler. Only the concrete pads, faded signs, and the rides' on and off ramps remained. It didn't take much to imagine the nostalgic music or the smell of popcorn and hot dogs.

If I survive, it would be fun to go to a very not-haunted, not-abandoned theme park with Gage. I bet we'd have a good time.

Thinking of Gage made him sad but determined. They might not make a go of their budding relationship for all kinds of reasons, but Scott was determined to live long enough to give it his best effort.

Horse barns, a dirt race track, and a grandstand loomed ahead as Scott followed the road farther into the old park. He knew that maintenance sheds and gates had to be on the outskirts, out of sight of guests. Maybe the service entrance would also be under guard, but he had to check. If that failed, perhaps he could find a break in the fence.

It's a big park, and I don't think the coyote pack is very large. They can't be everywhere, and I can move pretty fast.

Scott slipped past the rodeo area, still looking for an exit. He passed under an ornate iron archway that had large, gnarled trees on either side. Weathered Victorian-style houses with Mansard roofs and cupolas lined a stretch of road leading to a creepy mansion. He passed a fake cemetery with tombstones and mausoleums. The houses had signs that read Taxidermy, Potions and Poisons, Fortunes Told, and Macabre Merchandise.

A Haunted Mine sign pointed down a sloped road to the attraction. Beyond it, Scott glimpsed a service road and the tops of maintenance buildings, revealing the back exit.

He intended to go around the mine and head for the exit. Then he spotted three armed guards running toward him, pointing.

"Get him!" one of them shouted.

Scott glanced behind him and saw three more of the coyotes closing in. Desperate, he ran for the haunted mine attraction. Like everything else, it was fenced off, but the entrance to the ride itself was cracked and hung ajar.

With the coyotes closing from two directions, Scott knew he wouldn't make it out of the park without getting caught. Desperate, he jumped at the chain link and flipped himself over like he hadn't done since high school. He hit the ground running.

His head throbbed, and his vision blurred, but Scott kept going, afraid of what the coyotes would do if they caught him— either in their human or animal form. He broke down the door to the attraction and ventured into the dark interior.

The first room looked like the parlor of a Victorian mansion. Light filtered through the dirty, mullioned windows. Real dust lay thick on the high-backed couch that had been unstuffed where rats and squirrels had torn into it for bedding. Velvet curtains hung in shreds, and a water leak stained the patterned wallpaper.

Grimy candles still stood in an iron candelabra. Scott grabbed the base and ran, moving farther into the attraction. He heard the coyotes behind him and delved deeper.

He turned a corner, expecting to find more of the fake house's interior, only to discover he was in the queue for the haunted mine ride.

Shit. Too late to turn around now.

Scott plucked the candles from the candelabra and shoved them in his pocket, hoping they would still light. He dropped the heavy candelabra into the water and watched it sink, preferring the lighter and more maneuverable chair leg as a weapon.

He eyed the ride launch area, a pier with a line of shallow boats. Scott figured the vessels were on a track and useless without power. He spotted a narrow service walkway that wound into the shadows next to the wall and ran for it, hoping to be out of sight before the coyotes followed him.

His mouth tasted like stale water. The boat ride's lagoon was full and since it wasn't green with algae, he guessed it must have a natural source because any pumps or filters would have been turned off long ago.

Footsteps echoed, closer now.

Desperate, Scott followed the narrow ledge. As soon as it rounded a bend, the light faded. He stuck to the wall, using his hands to guide him and hoped the walkway didn't end abruptly or he would be swimming.

The deeper he went into the darkness, the more he smelled mold, mildew, and rats. Bad as it was, he hoped it masked his scent from his pursuers. The ledge would be difficult for them in their fur, and if they tried to chase him, they wouldn't be able to move faster than a shuffle without landing in the water.

Scott ignored the smell and moved as silently as he could manage.

Around the next bend he saw shadowy figures and froze. After a moment, he realized that faint sunlight filtered through holes in the roof, revealing a tableau of mannequins seated around a large dinner table. He crept closer and saw that the scene depicted a horrific feast.

Even though time, temperature, and rodents had taken a toll on the next scene, Scott could make out the details. A group of miners toiled in a mine with pickaxes, but behind them lurked menacing ghosts poised to strike.

Under other circumstances, Scott would have appreciated the macabre ride. Now, he doubted he would ever enjoy a haunted house in quite the same way again.

He swore he heard voices and footsteps echoing behind him and headed deeper into the attraction. The next scene depicted werewolves threatening campers in the woods, and the following set of a haunted campground showed rows of tombstones against a night sky with gauze stretched over wire forms rising from the graves. Time and disuse yellowed their shrouds, but their menace remained clear.

Scott passed several more vignettes depicting miners and settlers meeting a bloody end at the hands of all sorts of paranormal creatures.

A sharp, chemical taste in his mouth alerted Scott that something was off.

He went around a bend and stopped cold. The scene might originally have been a mad scientist's lab, but the props and set dressing had been removed, and he found himself staring at a real laboratory.

I've found where the coyotes are making at least some of their drugs. It's crazy genius. No one comes here. The ride might still have functioning electricity with a generator and natural gas or they figured out how to make it work. There's a water source close at hand. And they can use the boats to transport materials in and product out.

Shit. I might not live long enough to report them. I've got to do something myself.

Scott could hear his pursuers, and he didn't want to let them catch up. Enough light entered from the damaged roof that he didn't need to use a candle, which he hoped helped him hide in the gloomy interior. The ledge skirted the waterway where boats once carried passengers through the attraction.

Scott reached the next scene, a bonfire surrounded by dancing demons with four bound prisoners who were likely to become dinner or sacrifices. He spotted the control box that would allow natural gas to flow to the bonfire for realistic flames.

Footsteps closed in from the other direction now, and in a few minutes Scott would be trapped. He looked around wildly, hoping for inspiration. His hand closed on the pack of matches in his pocket as he considered the bonfire. It had been damaged, and some of the piping was exposed.

Scott jumped into the tableau, trying not to think too hard since his plan only looked good compared to the certainty of being caught. He unwound a length of rope from around his waist and set one end in place next to the burners and broken pipes of the fake bonfire, moved away, and lit the other end like a fuse.

Once he was certain the fire had taken on the rope, Scott found the control knob for the gas burners and opened it up. The smell of natural gas confirmed that the supply hadn't been completely depleted.

Scott took two strides toward the canal and dove in. He held his breath and sank, plugging his ears with his fingers.

Seconds later, the bonfire scene exploded, and a fireball expanded over the whole area before bringing down the ceiling.

Lungs bursting, Scott saw dancing lights in front of his eyes as he put his arms over his head. He stayed on the bottom beneath the water and hoped he hadn't colossally miscalculated.

Pieces of ceiling fell into the canal when the fireball cleared, and Scott sheltered next to one of the empty boats to dodge the debris that pelted down.

If I'm going to die, I'd rather die escaping. Those coyotes didn't intend anything good. I was probably going to end up in a shallow grave out in the woods. I didn't want it to end like this. I'm sorry that Gage and I didn't get the time together we wanted, and I'm sorry for the misunderstanding. I think I love him, and I'm pretty sure he was falling for me. He deserved a happy ending. I hope he won't forget me.

Self-preservation took over. As soon as the ceiling stopped falling, Scott stayed low in the water and used a combination of walking and swimming to navigate the shallow channel. He avoided the steaming chunks that floated on the surface and ignored the thought that nasty bacteria might have mutated in the water.

When he couldn't hold his breath any longer, Scott resurfaced. Smoke filled the tunnel, acrid with the smell of burning drugs and whatever the ride's sets had been made out of. He coughed and wheezed, hoping he didn't die from smoke inhalation or overdose on the drug fumes.

Still better than whatever the coyotes had planned for me. Not sure I'm going to make it out. I hope Gage can forgive me. My first—and probably last—case is likely to be a story they tell after I'm gone, at least as a cautionary tale. How many other agents blew up a mad scientist's lair and a vampire dungeon to finish the job?

After the smoke cleared, Scott dared to take a look around. It appeared that the blast had brought down enough of the ceiling to block the path ahead, so he grimly began trekking back the way he came and hoped that the coyotes who had been chasing him had fled for their lives.

That must have been the case because he didn't encounter any pursuers. He stopped to wring the water out of his sodden clothing and prayed that his shoes didn't squelch loudly enough to give him away.

It would be nice if they all just ran away because of the explosion. But I never have that kind of luck.

Scott sidestepped sections of ceiling and chunks of plaster to make his way back to the haunted house entrance. The blast had knocked over furniture, cracked walls, and shattered windows. It smelled like smoke, so he figured the blast had caught something down below on fire. That meant it was a good time to leave and take his chances on the outside.

Still clutching the chair leg, Scott eased his way out of the attraction's entrance, watching for threats. There was no sign of the smugglers who had pursued him, and he guessed they either fled or were trapped in the rubble.

I'm surprised I didn't get buried alive. Of course, I'm still stuck in the middle of the forest with the smugglers who didn't run away and miles from help with no phone. I'm definitely not out of the woods yet.

He shivered as the wind picked up, chilling him in his sodden clothing. *If I can't find shelter and dry clothes, hypothermia might finish what the smugglers started.*

Scott dodged into the mercantile and found a rain jacket and waterproof pants on a shelf near the register, still sealed in dusty, yellowed plastic. He pulled them on over his shirt and pants, glad for something to help preserve body heat and deflect the wind, even if it didn't rid him of his wet clothing.

Only then did he realize his hands shook, a combination of cold and a near-death experience. He took several deep breaths, trying to steady himself.

I'm not out yet, and there's no telling how many smugglers are still in the park. Plus I've got to get from wherever-this-is back to Fox Hollow. And then I'll apologize to Gage for not answering his texts. I've got a pretty good excuse.

Scott looked both ways before he ducked out of the shop and started to look for the perimeter fence. The main gate might be guarded, but he doubted the coyotes secured the fence around the whole area.

If the smugglers had moved into the old park, they hid their presence well. *Maybe they just used it to make the drugs and warehouse them.*

But that didn't make sense. The location was too remote and would attract attention if locals spotted people coming and going. His second guess was that there was a building being used as a barracks, and a small group of the coyotes lived and worked at the lab.

If they stayed largely in their coyote form, they could hunt for food, and they wouldn't need nearly as many supplies as humans.

The water in the boat ride had been fresh, so it had to have a nearby source. If a stream or river ran close to the park, the smugglers might be receiving shipments from Canada on the water and moving the product they produced by boat.

A remote area like this is hard for anyone to keep an eye on all the time. Too much land and not enough forest rangers.

The taste in his mouth shifted to stale cigarettes, a warning. *They didn't all run away or get blown up. I've got to get out of here before they catch me.*

"Stop right there." A man stepped out from the side of a building, pointing a rifle at Scott's heart. "Who sent you?"

Scott figured he was likely to die, and he didn't owe these creeps a straight answer. "Santa Claus. You've been very naughty."

The man cocked the rifle. "Wrong answer. Try again."

The sudden taste of chocolate and strawberries filled Scott's mouth as a huge animal bounded from between the buildings and chomped down hard on the gunman's wrist. Scott saw a large, solidly built black and brown dog pinning the gunman to the ground with a deep, vicious growl.

Scott dropped flat as the rifle fired a wild shot, and the man screamed in pain.

Gage. That's got to be Gage. He's fuckin' gorgeous.

Wolves howled, a bear roared, and a fox screamed. Something huge bellowed loudly seconds before an angry bull moose burst into view.

It took a moment for Scott to realize that he wasn't about to die.

This might be the strangest rescue in the world, but I think I might be okay after all.

CHAPTER 10
GAGE

Earlier that day.

Madden's intel from the squirrels and birds was right on point. They reported seeing scruffy men and actual coyotes coming and going from the old amusement park and occasionally from the deserted mining town.

One of the surveillance squirrels said he had seen the smugglers hustling an injured man into a building at the western park, and that was all Armel and Gage needed to hear to mobilize their team.

The good thing about being shifters was they all fit in one big SUV, even the moose. Madden drove separately and went ahead to rally the squirrels.

Sheriff Armel drove. Brandon navigated based on information provided by Madden. Gage sat with Liam, and the Lowe brothers took the rear seat. No one spoke on the trip, which took less than an hour.

Liam put a hand on Gage's arm and gave him an encouraging smile. Gage managed to smile back, but he knew it was weak and worried.

They pulled into the old park's lot, an expanse of faded asphalt with saplings growing through the cracks. Madden was already waiting for them, and Gage resolved to remember that the squirrel had a lead foot.

Gage hadn't expected to be met by hundreds of red and gray squirrels who hurried over like a tide. Madden hunkered down and listened to their chatter, then nodded and placed a hand over his heart in thanks. The squirrels drew back but didn't scatter.

He rose and turned to the others. "They saw Scott get loose and sneak into the haunted mine ride. And they also said the scruffy men came and went from there and brought boats out to the ride entrance where other people put boxes onto trucks."

"So they're making the drugs here," Russ Lowe said with a grim expression.

"Or using the materials that come down from Canada for last steps," his brother Drew pointed out.

"Please thank your friends," Gage told Madden. "We couldn't do this without them."

"Let's go fix this," Sheriff Armell said with a thunderous expression.

They shifted and left their clothing in the SUV. Russ had a special clip on his dog collar that let him carry the key fob and his cell phone, and Brandon carried a pack with useful equipment. Madden and the squirrels surged ahead, leading the way.

Gage took in the faded FrontierWorld sign and the old-timey style of the remaining buildings. While the rides had been removed and some of the buildings were in bad shape, others had remained remarkably well-preserved aside from peeling paint.

The bear and two wolf shifters led the way, with the squirrels streaming beside them. After that came Gage and Liam, with Brandon's moose bringing up the rear.

We are going to save our mate, his Mal said. *I am ready to bite.*

Just make sure you know who you're biting. Don't get carried away.

I won't—but if our mate is hurt, I will bite.

Gage couldn't blame his Malinois side for having strong opinions. Knowing that Scott was taken against his will and probably injured brought out all of Gage's deep-rooted protective instincts. He wanted to fight the bad guys and make the ones responsible for hurting Scott pay. He wanted to fix the misunderstanding between them so he could stay close to Scott for the rest of their lives and make sure nothing bad ever happened to him again.

We will keep him safe, his Mal vowed.

He's a government agent. We aren't going to be able to protect him all the time, Gage warned.

We should always be together. His inner Malinois had definite opinions.

I brew beer. I'm not cut out for being a secret agent. Remember? That's why we didn't go into the family business.

It hadn't just been human Gage who didn't want the military life. His Mal did fine with loud noises and excelled at agility training but had an unfortunate tendency to faint at the sight of blood. Not all the time, but even once would be a serious problem in a combat situation.

Get a little woozy and no one ever lets you forget it, his Mal grumbled.

We swooned like a Disney princess, Gage reminded his other half as they headed toward the location the squirrels had identified.

Only once.

That's okay, Gage soothed. *Today we need to be Scott's protector, and we can bite all the bad guys we can catch.*

An explosion shook the ground beneath their feet, deafeningly loud. Gage saw a plume of smoke and fire rise from a spot a little farther into the park, and he stared in horror as the squirrels shrieked.

Scott. Fuck. What just happened?

Alert for trouble, their posse headed in the direction of the explosion. They shifted the approach order so the bear and moose led the way, with the wolves next. Liam and Gage brought up the rear, although Gage had already arranged with Armell to take point once they closed in on Scott's location to utilize his tracking skills.

For now, the fireball in the sky gave them a pretty good idea of where Scott might be. Gage hoped that whatever caused the explosion, Scott was safe.

Coyotes burst into sight from everywhere. Half a dozen came running from the direction of the explosion. The bear sent one sprawling with a smack of his huge paw while the two wolves snapped and growled at another pair until the coyotes hunched in surrender. Squirrels hedged them in from all sides, and the moose reared, threatening to bring his hooves down on the coyotes, who cowered.

Gage spotted the old-time town jail and barked, leading the others inside, where a usable cell sat with an open door. Armel and the Lowe brothers shifted long enough to bind the coyotes with collars of silver chain that would keep them from changing back to human.

Gage nudged the door farther open and stood back, letting his friends herd the coyotes into the cell before swinging it shut. The bars were surprisingly solid, and Armel secured the cell door with more silver chain before he and the others shifted back.

Gage sprinted ahead, sure that Scott would be nearby. He relied on his mate bond to assure him Scott was still alive despite the explosion. As he neared the haunted mine ride, he sensed Scott not far ahead.

A big wooden building that had been the passenger intake and haunted house part of the ride blazed above a smoldering crater inside splintered wooden walls, open to the mechanical room below.

Farther on, Gage saw where boats came from beneath the building to float in a concrete canal that led to a stretch of land still decorated with figures of ghostly miners and frightening monsters.

The air smelled of smoke, burning wood, and an acrid chemical tang that suggested the smugglers had been using the building for their cargo. He heard voices up ahead and began to run, drawing on all the agility training his family had demanded in his childhood.

Our mate is in danger! We must protect.

Gage agreed with his Mal one hundred percent. As he came around the corner, he saw a scruffy man aiming a rifle at Gage, who was too close for the shot to miss. Instinct took over. Gage leaped, flying across the gap between him and the gunman, and snapped his powerful jaws shut on the man's wrist as they both tumbled to the ground.

The shot went wild, but Gage made sure the shooter remained pinned. He felt a surge of relief when he realized that he and Scott hadn't been shot.

The others were nearby. He heard their howls, shrieks, and roars as well as the unquestionable thunder of a loose moose. Brandon came barreling toward them and his broad antlers looked like they took up the entire width of the passageway. The bear followed in its wake while the fox, wolves, and squirrels hurried along behind them.

Gage didn't let go of the would-be shooter until the sheriff shifted back to human form, long enough to use silver handcuffs from Brandon's bag to bind the man and toss him over Brandon's back, face down like a sack of flour.

Gage spat to get the taste of blood out of his mouth. He nuzzled Scott's leg, sending his feelings through the mate bond.

Relief flooded through Gage, his own and what he sensed from Scott. The sight of Scott's bruised face and black eye raised a growl deep in Gage's chest. He eyed the shooter, thinking that perhaps he hadn't bitten hard enough since the man's hand was still attached.

"Down, boy." Scott gave a relieved laugh that bordered on hysteria as he struggled to sit up. "Is that you, Gage?"

Gage placed his front paws on Scott's shoulders and licked the undamaged side of his face.

"I'm glad to see you too." Scott scratched Gage's ears. "Looks like you brought the whole crew."

"Come on," the sheriff said. "You can tell us how you blew the roof off later. Before the rest comes tumbling down, let's get out of here. Can you walk?"

Gage growled. If Scott needed to ride Brandon, he would be fine with dragging the cuffed shifter along by the ankle.

"I think so," Scott told him. Armel shifted into his bear half, and they headed back toward where the rescue party had entered.

Gage stuck next to Scott, glued to his leg. *What about the bad shifters in the jail?* his Mal asked.

The sheriff will send someone back for them. Eventually, Gage told his other half.

There were so many things Gage wanted to say, so many questions he needed to ask.

Did you cause the explosion? Why did you blow up the ride? Are you hurt? Who hit you so I can chew on their leg?

Sometimes Gage disagreed with his Mal's very direct way of viewing the world, but when it came to dealing with the men who kidnapped Scott, he was all for leaving scars to remind them of their poor life choices.

When they got to the gate, an army of squirrels and birds were waiting for them. The guards Scott had glimpsed before were nowhere in sight.

"What the—" Scott took in the scene wide-eyed, but Gage would have to wait to explain it.

Scott looked at him. "One of your shifter friends did something?"

Gage nodded.

Despite everything Scott burst out laughing. "That's fuckin' awesome! This is the best Disney rescue *ever*!"

The bear snorted and tossed his head but still managed to look amused.

"Don't worry—I won't break into song," Scott added. That he could still crack jokes eased the cold fear that had gripped Gage since Scott disappeared.

He figured his boyfriend would crash later when the adrenaline faded, and would need to deal with the trauma after things settled. But for now, Scott was able to walk out, his injuries appeared to be superficial, and they had the bad guys in custody.

No win was ever perfect, but this came pretty close.

Back at the vehicles, the rescuers shifted and dressed. Sheriff Armel called a friend in the FBSI located in Lake George and explained the situation, asking for backup to take the shifters into custody. Brandon, Liam, and Russ went back to the jail with guns to keep an eye on the coyotes, while the Sheriff and Drew intended to stay with the SUV to wait for the FBSI to arrive.

They threw the handcuffed coyote into the cargo area of the SUV none too gently, and he landed with a quiet *oof*. Scott left a message for April about capturing the coyotes and destroying the lab, plus turning the drug runners over to paranormal law enforcement. This time he was able to get through to her voicemail and leave a full message without a problem.

Madden had driven separately, so he agreed to take Scott and Gage to the hospital in Fox Hollow once Gage made quick introductions and they had thanked the squirrels and birds.

"How are you doing, Scott?" Madden asked as he drove, sparing a glance in the rearview mirror to the back seat where Scott and Gage clung to one another like they would never let go.

"Better—now." Scott sounded a little shaky. "Thank you all for coming for me."

"Seems like you did a pretty good job rescuing yourself,"

Madden said. "That was one hell of a distress signal you sent up!"

"I didn't expect it to be quite such a big explosion," Scott admitted. "But all I had was a pack of matches, so I needed to improvise."

"Scared the shit out of the squirrels, but at least they knew where to find you," Madden added.

"Please give them my thanks. You had a big posse back there."

Madden grinned. "They enjoyed it. It can get boring, sitting around staring at your nuts." The twinkle in his eye made it clear the double meaning was intentional.

"Kind of a shame about the park itself," Gage said. "I bet it was fun for kids back in the day. Sorry to see those places close."

Scott shivered. "I think it's going to be a long, long time before I watch another western."

Gage and Scott held hands tightly. They sat pressed together from hip to knee, bumping shoulders. Gage's Mal drank in Scott's scent, and the connection of the mate bond comforted them.

Gage turned to him, thinking of all the things he wanted to say when they were alone. *I missed you. I worried about you. Don't ever leave. I love you.*

That would wait until they were back in Fox Hollow and a doctor had treated Scott for his injuries. Gage hadn't noticed Scott moving like he was hurt, but he didn't know if there had been other damage.

"I have no idea how I'm going to write this up in my case notes." Scott sighed. "Then again, I get the impression that a lot of the agents at SPAM aren't exactly *conventional*."

"You did pretty well," Gage pointed out. "Nabbed the bad guys, blew up the lab, and burned their inventory."

"I'm betting that when the feds pick up those coyotes in the jail, they'll tell everything they know about the Canadian connection," Madden said from the front.

"If they had a lab here, they weren't moving finished product as much as raw materials. Knowing that will help the rangers and customs folks look for the right leads. This will go a long way toward shutting down their operation—at least, in this area," Gage chimed in. "And the sheriff put the feds wise to that abandoned mining town, so that's a second bust."

Gage had overheard enough conversations in his family to know that most of the time, the bad guys who didn't get caught just packed up shop and moved elsewhere instead of going away for good. Still, disrupting their channels and deliveries could make it expensive or impossible for the smugglers to continue. They might clear out and leave. While they were likely to just find another location, it still felt like a win that they wouldn't still be *here.*

Our mate is safe. Our friends were brave. No one is badly hurt. It is a good day, his Mal proclaimed proudly.

And you're awesome, Gage told his other half. He swore he could feel the Mal blush under his fur.

We have him back. That's what matters.

Gage squeezed Scott's hand and shifted slightly closer, anchoring them both in the knowledge that they were together, and the nightmare was over.

"I'm going to take Scott to the hospital so he can get checked out," Madden said.

Gage had already contacted his team at the taproom to let them know he wouldn't be in tonight and to handle the evening without him. He didn't have any events or tastings, so the others could take care of anything that came up.

He had no intention of letting Scott out of his sight—or his arms—for the foreseeable future.

"Come to the hospital with me, please," Scott said quietly. "I think I'm okay, but I'd feel better if you were with me."

Gage leaned in to press a quick kiss to his cheek, hoping there would be an opportunity to show Scott later just how much he missed him. "I have no intention of going anywhere without you," he promised. *Ever, if I have anything to say about it.*

Mate. Forever, his Mal agreed.

"Good—because I want us together," Scott said. "We'll figure out the details once I get over my near-death experience."

Madden drove straight to the hospital. He let Gage and Scott out and promised to be in touch after they got settled.

Scott kept a tight grip on Gage's hand as they walked into the building and went to the admissions desk.

The intake nurse didn't ask why they were there. "We were expecting you." Either she was psychic—a real possibility here—or Armel called ahead and told them what to expect. She looked at Gage. "Are you related? If not, we have a nice waiting area just down the hall."

Gage opened his mouth, but Scott beat him to it. "He's my boyfriend, and I really want to have him with me."

The nurse shrugged. "As long as he has your permission and doesn't interfere with the examination, that's up to you."

She ushered them into a waiting room and promised that someone would be with them shortly, then left and closed the door behind her.

Alone with each other for the first time since the rescue, Scott choked back a sob. His hands shook, and Gage could feel how hard the other man's heart pounded.

Gage wrapped his arms around him. "It's okay. Just let it all process. You can cry, or yell, or sit quietly. Whatever you need— I'm here." Gage's experience with a military and law enforcement family gave him insight into the aftermath of trauma.

"Thank you," Scott managed. "I knew that you and the sheriff would look for me, but when they took me to that old park, I didn't know how you'd find me."

"Good thing lots of people in this town are psychic." Gage forced a smile. "Everyone pulled together as soon as I told them what happened. This is a pretty awesome place."

Scott nodded, still struggling with his raw emotions. "Yeah. It is. And you're amazing. All I could think about besides getting free was that I couldn't die because I hadn't told you I love you."

Gage caught his breath before his brain came back online to respond. "I figured out that I love you too."

"I know it's fast, and we have a lot of getting to know each other to do," Scott went on as if he needed to fill the silence, "but I want more with you. I'll talk to my office when this is over and move to a place where we don't have as far between us."

"Do you think they'd let you move to Fox Hollow?" Gage asked. "Maybe you can sell them on the proximity to Canada without putting the town on the government's radar."

"We'll think of something. SPAM already seemed to know a little about the shifter side, and the Fox Institute and the psychics have been pretty famous for over a century," Scott pointed out. "I can figure out something. My boss, April, seems tough but open-minded. And if it doesn't work out, there's a taproom where I might be able to bus tables."

Gage leaned over and kissed him. "I am all in favor of nepotism, but I bet you can get a transfer to work out. After all, aren't they supposed to be psychic?"

"Good point."

A man in a white coat came in just then. "Scott?" he asked, and Scott nodded. "I'm Doctor Dunn. I hear you've had an unusual last few days."

"This is my partner," Scott said before the doctor could ask. "I want him to stay. It'll help me be calmer to talk about what happened."

Gage's Mal was braced for a fight, but the doctor just shrugged. "As long as you sign a permission waiver, it's fine with me." He handed off a clipboard and pen with a form, and Gage suspected the man had been warned ahead of time about their request.

Scott skimmed the document, signed it, and handed the board back.

"Now that the paperwork is done, how are you feeling?"

"My head hurts, my chest feels funny, and I'm groggy, but at the same time, super-twitchy," Scott reported.

"Okay, that gives me an idea of where to start. What happened?"

"Someone hit me over the head and knocked me out in the parking lot. When I came around the next day, I was tied up inside one of the old rides at the abandoned frontier park. I think they drugged me. I managed to get out of the ropes," Scott replied.

"I blew up a meth lab and hid underwater in the old haunted mine ride until the fireball passed overhead. Some of the ceiling must have fallen on me."

The doctor blinked once, then twice. Gage could see the man struggled to keep his professional demeanor. "I'm sorry. I thought you said—"

"He did. It's been a very strange day," Gage said. His Mal stirred, restless, and Gage struggled to tell his other half that the doctor was not a threat and might be a helper.

He doesn't understand. He isn't helping, his Mal fretted.

He doesn't have to know everything. Just enough to make Scott feel better. You can't bite him.

I want to.

You can't. We live here. We might need to come back to the hospital someday.

The doctor recovered quickly. "All right, then. Let's have a look at you." He gestured for Scott to get on the examining table while Gage took a seat along the wall where he could make encouraging eye contact with Scott.

Gage's Mal paced in his mind as the doctor examined Scott. *Dude. Sit down. You're driving me nuts. You'd be wearing a groove in the floor by now.*

I'm worried about our mate. And I still want to bite the bad man.

The sheriff will take care of the bad man. You already nearly bit his hand off. And by the way, eww. Blood tastes bad. I probably need a shot.

His Mal preened. *Maligator!*

The doctor poked and prodded Scott, checking his sight and reflexes and gently touching the back of his head. He examined the rope chafing and the small burns, swabbed Scott's nose and throat, listened to his breathing, and took a blood sample.

"I'm going to have them take you down to the lab to run a few more tests, and I'll be back to discuss the results. Sit tight and try to relax. It sounds like you deserve it." With that, he left them alone. The examining room seemed unnaturally quiet after all the excitement.

A nurse wheeled Scott out of the room for more tests, promising Gage they would be back soon. Gage paced until Scott returned.

"How do you feel?" Gage had an inkling through the mate bond, but he thought conversation might take Scott's mind off what had happened.

"Honestly? I think I'm in shock. That sets in afterward, right? I'm beginning to think that there's a lot SPAM didn't cover in their Introduction to Being a Supe class. I guess I shouldn't be surprised—it was a slideshow with Q&A."

Gage frowned. "You're sure this SPAM thing is a legit government organization? It sounds really hinky."

"I don't think they have a big budget since they're secret and all," Scott replied. "Orientation lasted two weeks. They gave me a gun and let me shoot at the range, took all my biometrics, had me fill out a will and organ donor form, and gave me a badge. We had several slideshows. There was a quiz at the end."

Gage looked at him hoping that Scott was kidding. He hadn't gone military himself, but he was well aware of the training his family members underwent for various branches. When he realized Scott wasn't joking, Gage managed a polite smile. "How long have you been an agent?"

Scott sighed. "This was my first case. I hope they won't hold the explosion against me."

Gage's Mal growled, angry that their mate had been sent into danger with questionable training. *They cover more than that in obedience school.*

We didn't go to obedience school, Gage pointed out. *I wonder if I joined SPAM would they let Scott and me partner?*

He needs us to keep him safe, his Mal agreed.

We'll figure that out—later, Gage replied.

Two nurses came in with a cart that held tools and equipment. "While Doc waits on test results, we're going to treat those open wounds." The speaker was a motherly sort who reminded Gage of someone he once worked with. "This won't take long."

They cleaned Scott's wrists, making sure to get all of the rope fibers, and covered the raw, red wounds with salve before wrapping them in gauze. "That should start feeling better pretty soon."

The older nurse took a different tube from the tray and applied a dab to each of the small burns caused by the flaming debris. "This will help the pain and speed healing. If any of these look red or get more sore, tell us. You don't want them to get infected. Burns can be tricky." Finally, she handed him a bottle of water. "Stay hydrated. Water heals almost everything, and getting dehydrated slows down your recovery."

He thanked her and sat down next to Gage again. "Guess I've given everyone something exciting to talk about." He gently touched the gauze that wrapped his wrists.

"We don't get explosions every day if that's what you mean." Gage tried to lighten Scott's mood. "I imagine it'll be the talk of the town until something else comes along."

They sat together in comfortable silence for a while. The door opened, and the doctor came back inside, along with a nurse. "We have your lab results."

Gage and Scott sat up, braced for bad news, and Scott reached for Gage's hand.

"You have bruising on the back of your skull and a mild concussion—not surprising if you were hit hard enough to knock you out," Dr. Dunn said. "But the X-rays show no skull fracture, so that's good."

"No surprise you are dehydrated. We also found strong traces of a sedative in your blood. It should wear off in a day, but you'll want to avoid alcohol and similar medications until then. I suggest lots of liquids."

Dr. Dunn consulted his notes. "I'm putting you on an antibiotic because we turned up odd bacteria when we swabbed your nose. We don't know what contaminants might have been in the water at the park, so it's best to put you on something that will knock out the most likely culprits. It's easier to get in front of an infection like that than try to play catch-up after it takes hold. And something for the pain, because those bruises are going to ache, and so will your head."

Gage made sure to pay close attention because while Scott was nodding and looking at the doctor, Gage felt certain he wasn't registering most of what was being said.

"I also had a witch do a full body and blood scan since we didn't know the capabilities of the coyotes. She thinks they used a spell along with the drugs to knock you out, but because of your ability, it didn't last as long as they expected." He looked up from his notes.

"I know you're not from Fox Hollow, but I'm still going to write you a script for some trauma counseling. We have folks here who can do sessions online, so you could speak freely to someone who understands about shifters and paranormal abilities," Dr. Dunn added. "That way, you can focus on talking about what you feel and not have to censor what you say." He smiled. "Even badass superheroes need some counseling now and then."

"What about everything else?" Scott asked. "When can I resume...normal activities?" he asked, and his eyes flickered toward Gage.

"I'd suggest taking it easy for the next couple of days as far as running, climbing, and very strenuous activities," Dr. Dunn replied. "If something hurts, stop doing it. I wouldn't do anything that shakes you around a lot—so you might want to avoid roller coasters for the time being. We also tell folks to avoid screen time for the first couple of days. Limit your phone use and avoid television and computers.

"Pretty much everything else is okay—as long as it doesn't cause pain," the doctor concluded. "There's no reason to avoid other regular activities, but I'd save anything particularly *acrobatic* until later." He gave them a look that was as clear a permission slip for sex as Gage figured they were going to get.

<hr>

"HOW ARE YOU, REALLY?" Gage asked once Scott received the paperwork to go home. Gage walked out to the car shoulder-to-shoulder with Scott after carefully scanning the parking lot for threats.

"We're back in Fox Hollow. I think we're safe now," Scott said, with fond humor at Gage's protectiveness.

"Someone kidnapped you *from* Fox Hollow, so it's not *that* safe," Gage growled.

"Down boy." Scott pressed a kiss to Gage's cheek. "I adore your Malinois, but I think you're taking it a little too far."

Gage realized that he was walking in front of Scott like a bodyguard and tried to relax.

"I couldn't protect you before. I'm not going to let anyone get you now." But he stepped back and to the side to walk next to Scott.

Scott took his arm. "And I wouldn't want it any other way, but I'm not getting any premonition that the coyotes are around." Gage understood that meant Scott wasn't picking up on any tastes that warned him about impending danger.

"If my Malinois had his way, you'd be in protective custody," Gage replied, trying to relax.

Hearing the litany of injuries Scott had sustained strained

Gage's temper, even if he had been part of the rescue and had permanently injured one of Scott's attackers. He knew it could have been much worse, but that was cold comfort.

Human Gage knew he did his best, rallying the Fox Hollow crew, recruiting Madden's squirrel spies, and cluing in to the location. Malinois Gage faulted himself for every bruise and scrape and for whatever subsequent trauma Scott suffered.

"Hey," Scott said quietly. "Let it go. Please? I'm here. We're together. We're okay."

Gage nodded, still struggling to step back from the emotions that raged in both sides of him. Scott was the first person he had ever felt so strongly about, and he wasn't used to coping with his own fears in addition to his Mal's instinctive need to protect.

"Where do you want to go?" Gage helped Scott into his truck. He realized that Scott only had his motel room, which probably felt unsafe after the attack.

Scott hesitated, and Gage realized that they hadn't cleared the air between them despite the rescue.

"I understand why you didn't tell me right away about the secret agent stuff," Gage said. "But my feelings were hurt in the moment, and I didn't react well. Then you went missing, and I went nuts trying to find you. I'm sorry."

"I'm sorry too," Scott said. "I didn't mean to deceive you. I'm still new at this, and I wasn't sure what to do. I should have trusted you faster. I didn't mean to hurt you. But I was miffed because you got mad, and I didn't want to respond when I was still out of sorts, which was why I didn't check my voicemails or call you back. I was planning to do it in the morning and everything went sideways."

"Think we can have a do-over?" Gage asked, still trying to quell the mix of fear and relief in his gut.

"I'd like that," Scott replied, with a charmingly shy smile for someone who just blew up a theme park. "Can we go to your place, please?" Scott asked. "I don't want to go back to the motel."

We probably couldn't anyhow since it's technically a crime scene.

"That's fine. I'll ask the sheriff when I can go over and get your things and your Pilot," Gage said. "You can stay with me as long as you want."

When they got to the cabin, Gage looked at Scott. "How long has it been since you've eaten?"

Scott had to think about it. "Since yesterday dinner."

Gage gave him a quick kiss. "So it's been too long since your meal. You need some food, or you'll feel crappy, and it won't be the concussion."

He got Scott settled on the sofa with comfortable pillows. "They said no TV," Gage added apologetically. "I can put on music."

"That's okay. Quiet is good. Even though I was underwater when the explosion happened, I can't hear as well as usual. I'm hoping that will go away. I forgot to ask at the hospital," Scott admitted.

"Sit here and contemplate the universe for a moment while I put a casserole in the oven," Gage said. "I hope you like cheeseburger macaroni. I made it ahead of time to pop in the oven when I got home from work."

"Love it," Scott said. "And now that you mention it, I'm starved."

"It's going to take a while to cook, but I can take your mind off being hungry," Gage promised with a wink.

"I can think of some ways to pass the time," Scott answered in a voice that went straight to Gage's balls.

Gage set the oven and put in the casserole, then hurried back to where Scott waited.

"If you're up to letting me give you a sponge bath around your bandages, I can lay out clean clothes for you to borrow— they probably won't quite fit, but they'd make you feel better," Gage offered. He wanted to have the chance to check over every inch of his boyfriend to assure himself that Scott was okay, but he realized that his partner might want a little time alone to decompress.

"Thank you. I need to get the hospital smell and the sweat off me," Scott said. "But I…I don't want to be alone."

Gage grinned. "I thought you'd never ask."

He adjusted the water, checked the soap and shampoo, and tried not to stare when Scott got undressed, looking for injuries.

Bruises bloomed on Scott's shoulder and hip, probably from where he fell after being hit on the head or rough handling by the coyotes during transport. The back of Scott's head had a bump that looked tender, and the cuts and contusions on his face were still livid.

"I want to touch you," Scott told him. "I need you to hold me, ground me, help me believe I got out of there. Please, help me let go."

Gage took Scott into his arms, and for several moments, they stood entwined, just soaking up each other's presence. Gage held him tightly, letting Scott rest his head on his shoulder and bury his face in his neck.

Scott stood where he was out of the direct spray, letting Gage gently wipe him down with a soapy washcloth, getting rid of the grime and the smell of antiseptics. He sighed in contentment when Gage washed his hair, adding a scalp massage. As the water rinsed away, it seemed to take some of his stress and fear with it. Gage took a couple of minutes to wash himself, needing to sluice away the bad memories.

Getting clean relaxed both of them, and Gage hoped that it helped to restore Scott's sense of safety. Optimistically, they both cleaned well everywhere. "I was afraid I'd never see you again," Scott murmured. "I'm still afraid that if I shut my eyes this will all be a dream and I'll be back there, in the ride."

Gage turned off the shower and guided Scott out, grabbing his fluffiest towel to dry him. He daubed gently at the bruises and worked around the bandages. When Scott was dry, Gage hung up the towel and continued with gentle touches, reassuring them both.

Gage slowly let his hands roam over Scott's body. He started at the shoulders, tracing his palms down both arms, careful to avoid the burns and rope cuts, then splayed his hands across Scott's chest and back, confirming and worshiping.

"I want you," Scott said. "Fuck me, and help me believe I'm safe and alive."

"The doctor said—"

"As long as we don't have sex while riding a roller coaster, we're okay," Scott paraphrased. "That's what I got out of it."

"I like your translation." Gage figured if Scott could joke, he hadn't been completely overwhelmed by the shadow of the events.

"Dinner should be done by now," Gage said. "Let's eat, and then we can pick up where we left off in the bedroom." He handed Scott the pair of sleep shorts and top he had set out and waited for him to get dressed.

Dinner was a necessary afterthought since their minds were on finishing what they had started in the shower. The comfort food hit the spot, warm and filling, and they ate more than usual since they had both missed meals. Afterward, it didn't take long for Gage to put away leftovers and lock up for the night.

"I didn't have time to tidy the place. I haven't been back since I found out you were missing," Gage admitted. "I'm not always this messy."

They moved into the bedroom, and Gage laid Scott back on the mattress, taking care not to jostle his head, and climbed on to straddle him. This wasn't the high-energy sex he had pictured before their tiff and the kidnapping, but Gage knew that they would have their chance at that eventually.

What mattered was taking care of Scott in every way. Gage laid down next to Scott, letting their hands and mouths explore.

"How do you want it?" Gage asked between kisses.

"Think I'd better stay on my back this time," Scott replied. "So how about I let you have your way with me?"

"I like the sound of that." Gage worked his way down Scott's neck with his lips and tongue and explored his nipples, figuring out what made his lover shiver. He kissed his way down Scott's treasure trail and moved lower, with a hand firmly gripping each ass cheek.

Scott drew his knees up, opening himself to Gage's exploration. Gage paused to reach for a tube of lube stashed beneath the pillow.

"If anything doesn't feel good or you just want me to stop, say so," Gage warned, raising his head to meet Scott's eyes. "We can always do things at another time or not do them at all if it's something you don't like."

"I promise I'll tell you. Now get going before I die of blue balls." Scott sounded breathless.

Gage spread Scott wide and dove in, eating him out with gusto. Scott yelped at the first touch of Gage's tongue, and Gage felt a surge of possessive satisfaction at the thought that perhaps Scott hadn't done this often with other lovers.

Mate.

They were both in their thirties, so Gage hadn't expected a virgin lover and certainly wasn't one himself. Still, he had been picky about who he had taken to his bed outside of brief hand jobs or hurried, desperate blow jobs. He had only shared this side of himself with a few people, ones he trusted not to take advantage of his vulnerability.

Now, he tried to use everything he had experienced to pleasure Scott, with the addition of a few techniques he had learned from videos. Gauging by the moans and squirming, Scott seemed to be enjoying the effort.

Once he had Scott relaxed and a little looser, Gage slicked up a finger and pressed inside. Scott gave a surprised yelp and lifted his hips, spreading his legs to welcome the intrusion.

Gage turned his attention to Scott's dripping cock and tight balls while his finger moved in and out of Scott's tight hole.

"Please," Scott begged.

"You're not ready yet," Gage said, pulling off. "I want to make this real good for you. Let me get you open," he added with a wink.

Gage added a second finger and made sure he found Scott's magic spot, leaving him gasping. "You look so good like this," Gage told him. "So sexy."

He reached down to adjust himself since he was painfully hard. "Don't think we're going to last long this first time."

"Come on. Don't make me wait."

Once a third finger moved in and out easily, Gage's patience found its end. He reached for the lube and paused.

"We should have talked about this sooner, but rubber or no rubber? I get tested regularly, and I'm negative."

"Haven't been with anyone since my last test, and I'm negative, too. Now fuck me!"

"Toppy bottom," Gage said with a laugh. He lined himself up and pushed in slowly, giving Scott time to adjust.

He loved the sounds of pleasure Scott made and the trust he showed surrendering himself to Gage. This wasn't the time for anything exotic, but Gage looked forward to trying new things together once they had a chance to get used to each other and recover from the kidnapping.

For now, it was enough to hear the sounds Gage's fingers and tongue drew from Scott and feel how Scott's hole clenched around his cock. He tried to take it as slow as he could, hoping their first time together would be memorable. Gage took hold of Scott's cock, already wet with pre-come, and began to stroke him to match his rhythm.

Scott came apart under him, shaking and calling out Gage's name and clenching his fists in the sheet as he arched up into Gage's thrusts, driving his cock deeper. Gage increased his pace and felt his climax rushing up, sweeping over him in a mix of emotions.

Ribbons of jizz painted Scott's chest, neck, and chin as he climaxed, and Scott followed him over the edge seconds later, nearly whiting out from the intensity.

They lay tangled together for several minutes until they could think and breathe again.

"Guess we need another shower," Scott said. They were slick with sweat and come, flushed with pleasure, hearts still thudding.

"Unless we want to stick together, and not in a good way," Gage replied. He pulled out gently and reached for the bedside box of tissues to mop up most of the jizz that had pooled on Scott's chest and beneath his ass.

"How about you get the water warm again while I change the sheets, and then I'll jump in to get both of us cleaned up again?" Gage said, leaning in to press his lips to Scott's. He tried to pour everything he felt into the kiss—love, relief, joy, and desire, and his heart leaped when Scott returned it with equal fervor.

When they finally broke apart, Gage felt lightheaded, something he thought only happened in romance books.

"Wow," he whispered.

Scott's grin held love, affection, and mischief. "Damn right, wow." He groaned. "But you've gotta move because I can't breathe."

Gage scrambled off, tumbling to one side. "Glad I took your breath away," he teased.

"Hold that thought."

It didn't take Gage long to strip the sheets and replace them. When he joined Scott in the shower for the second time that evening, he found him leaning against the wall out of the spray, arms wrapped around himself and shaking, even though the water was nearly scalding.

Gage turned the temperature down and approached Scott carefully. "Hey. It's me. You okay?"

Scott shook his head and gripped himself tighter.

"All right. I'm going to rinse myself super fast and wipe you down again, and then I'll get us dried off and take care of you," Gage promised. He knew that everything from the day would hit; he just didn't know when, and it seemed that reckoning was now.

Gage soaped up and let the spray sluice away the sweat and jizz, used a washcloth to help Scott freshen up, then turned off the water and reached for the towels. He gentled Scott away from the wall and rubbed him down, trying to drive away the chill even though he suspected it had nothing to do with the temperature. Once Scott was dry and no longer shaking, Gage toweled them both off fast and guided Scott out of the enclosure.

"Sit here, and I'll get clothes," he said, helping Scott sit on the edge of the tub.

Gage hurried back with the sweatpants and a soft T-shirt. He helped Scott balance as he pulled the pants on and maneuvered his arms into the shirt.

"How come I feel a little drunk, and I didn't drink?" Scott sounded adorably sleepy, but Gage listened to make sure he didn't slur his words, which would be a sign that the concussion was worse.

"Because you got smacked on the head." Gage guided Scott back to the freshly remade bed. He held out a hand with Scott's evening pills and the glass of water he had placed at the bedside.

"Take these. They'll help with the pain and get you to sleep. I'll be here if you need anything," Gage promised.

"You take good care of me," Scott murmured.

"That's what you do when you love someone." Gage leaned in to kiss Scott on the top of the head.

He watched to make sure Scott took his medicine, placed the glass on the nightstand, and helped get Scott into bed, kissing him gently on the lips.

"I'm going to go check the locks, and then I'll be in so we can sleep together," Gage told him when Scott patted the empty side of the bed.

"Want you close," Scott pouted.

"I will be close, but I need to make sure everything is set for the night. I won't be long."

Gage kissed him again and made the rounds, assuring himself everything was secure. Although the coyote problem had been solved—at least for now—Gage intended to speak to the sheriff about how to ensure that they had, in fact, eliminated the smuggling risk.

He had seen enough thriller movies to know that even James Bond never got *all* the bad guys. Movie sequels were good, but Gage had no interest in living through a repeat of today's drama.

If I can't deal with it, can we make a go of this? After all, he is a secret agent. If he wants to stay with SPAM, this sort of thing goes with the territory. Do they ever do less dangerous work? Like white collar embezzlement or fashion forgery? I guess it's going to depend on what Scott wants to do when he's had a chance to think about it. Am I cut out to love a spy? Could I live with that? Because I don't think I can live without him.

CHAPTER 11
SCOTT

Yes, ma'am. No, ma'am. Thank you, ma'am. Yes, I understand. Still terrifying, but it does make me feel a little better." Scott ended his call with April and looked at Gage.

"Well? What did she say?" Gage wanted to know. His inner Mal's tail swished back and forth impatiently, and his ears twitched.

"I'm getting a commendation despite the explosion. I guess I did better than some of the more seasoned agents who got caught without backup. I'm sure it helped that I didn't have to report losing my gun and badge since the sheriff found my stuff when they did the site cleanup."

Scott was surprised how much better he felt after just a day, thanks to medication, magic, sex, and a good night's sleep. "In fact, I didn't get the feeling they thought the explosion was a bad thing. More of a bonus round. She didn't share details, but their phone systems and AI were hacked. Reading between the lines, it involved a disgruntled employee, magic, and a confusion spell."

"Okay." Gage drew out the syllables. "And?

"April approved me moving to Fox Hollow," Scott said with

a grin. "Turns out they're aware of the Fox Institute and thought it would be good cover for me."

His smile slipped. "Unless that's too fast? If you're not okay—"

Gage wrapped his arms around Scott and nearly took him off his feet before planting a kiss on his lips. "Of course I'm okay with it! You can live with me, or we could have separate places until you're more comfortable. My Mal says you're our mate, so I'm not going anywhere."

"It's early days, but we could give living together a trial run. And if we need more elbow room or time, we can figure it out from there."

"How about the whole spy thing?" Gage sounded anxious.

"As it turns out, SPAM also investigates white-collar and financial crime," Scott says. "I told her about how when I was working for one company, I always got a dirty penny taste in my mouth whenever the financial director came around. Turns out he was cooking the books. That will only work when my cover as a food reviewer fits. I might still have to travel from time to time, but she was hopeful it would involve fewer explosions."

"Fewer? Not none?"

Scott nodded. "I guess there's always a chance."

"Okay," Gage relented. "I'll take my wins where I can get them. What else?"

"They think Jennings Weston—the witch—died in the explosion, but he's a slippery fellow given his magic, and they aren't entirely certain. So if he's not dead he might show up again, but they think he'll lie low for a while."

"Let's hope it's a very long while, and he moves far, far away," Gage said.

"Along with the commendation comes a raise and a promotion," Scott added. "They promoted me from Associate Special Agent to full Special Agent. Maybe I should blow things up more often."

Gage put a hand over his heart dramatically. "Please, no.

There has to be another way to move up in the organization or people would have flattened all of northern New York."

"And Dr. Jefferies left a message," Scott said. "I emailed him about classes that might help me understand my abilities better since I'll admit SPAM's orientation was a bit light on the details."

Gage looked like he was holding back on a more pointed opinion but didn't share his thoughts. Scott suspected he already knew, given his boyfriend's initial reaction to his nearly non-existent on-boarding.

"Jeffries says they have several classes and that there are psychics on staff who would do an independent study with me," Scott said. "And I figured I could volunteer at a certain taproom to use my superpower for good instead of evil as a taster on your new batches."

Gage grinned. "I already put a stipend for an official consultant in the new budget."

"Do I get that on a T-shirt?"

"I can make that happen if you want."

"Before this SPAM stuff, I had hoped to open a small plates kitchen or food truck someday," Scott said. "Maybe down the line, we could add to the taproom menu—if you like the idea."

"I think that would be a great addition. There are all kinds of things we can do," Gage said enthusiastically, which made Scott's heart soar.

Scott nodded, then winced. "I've got to quit moving my head like that." He touched the bump on the back gingerly with his fingertips.

"The doc said it would take a little while to go away, even with ice," Gage reminded him. "Does it hurt?"

"Only when I move my head," Scott replied.

"I'm doing a First Responders' Night at the taproom as well as a Squirrel Appreciation Night," Gage said. "That way we can thank everyone who was involved in the rescue. Liam is helping me with a hazelnut-flavored brew."

"I can't thank any of you enough for coming to save me,"

Scott said. "And everyone says you were the one who sounded the alarm and rallied the troops."

Gage blushed as his inner Mal preened. "I wasn't going to let those coyotes get away with it. You're my mate. I have to keep you safe."

"That goes both ways," Scott replied. "I protect you too. But I'll try to keep the explosions to a minimum."

THE TAPROOM WAS PACKED for First Responder Night. All first responders got their first drink free and a discount on subsequent drinks. Scott repeated his thanks to the group, even if he couldn't give details about his work.

"Everyone seems to be having a great time." Liam caught up with Scott at the bar. Liam and Madden were honorary first responders due to their roles in the rescue. Brandon and the Lowe brothers were Fox Hollow volunteer firefighters.

"I'm glad," Scott replied. "I owe everyone for saving my ass."

Liam met his gaze and cocked his head as if the statement didn't quite compute. "That's what friends do."

Scott knew the others understood how special Fox Hollow was, especially those like Liam who hadn't grown up there.

"I'm looking forward to your Library Night," Scott told him.

"It's a fundraiser, where a percentage of each drink price goes toward our book fund," Liam replied. "And we'll have a table with a display of our newest books and a wishlist for people who are willing to just buy books for us outright. The Fox Hollow library is small, but we have an impressive collection—not just the number of books but what we have for different ages and interests."

"Gage speaks highly about what you've done with the library," Scott replied.

"The library was already strong when I came into the position," Liam deflected, although he blushed. "I'm honored to be able to continue the legacy."

"I heard about the new exhibit about the area's defunct theme parks," Scott said.

"I can't wait to debut it," Liam replied with an enthusiastic glint in his eyes. "A lot of the folks in Fox Hollow have lived here their whole lives, so they remember the parks in their heyday."

"I wish I could have seen FrontierWorld under better circumstances," Scott said. "I bet it was fun."

"Russ and Drew remember it from when they were kids, and they thought it was great," Liam said. "But it's not the only park we've lost. There used to be a big water slide place and a very strange UFO-themed attraction, as well as a real Atlas missile silo."

"Wow. But I guess that's not a surprise—the Adirondacks have been a tourist attraction for a long time," Scott said, "Wasn't there also a Gay Nineties place?"

Liam smirked. "Yeah. All very Vegas-style stage shows and ice skating extravaganzas. And there was a Mother Goose park. So I think the presentation will stir up a lot of nostalgia."

He gave Scott a sly wink. "And it's also given me ideas for Halloween and Christmas. We have lots of places that are reputed to be haunted and plenty of mediums who can debunk the fakes and share their own stories about the real ones.

"For Christmas, those lost parks all did special displays and attractions with Santa and dancing elves and reindeer. I'm putting out a call to gather archival footage and family photos, plus stories of people who worked there or visited. I think it'll be a real winner," Liam said excitedly.

"And when people come in to see the display, we'll give them a chance to donate to the book fund," Liam added. "You haven't been here during the winter yet, but books keep people sane in these parts when the snow falls."

"I can't wait to feel like a real Fox Hollow resident," Scott said.

"We saved you. That makes you official," Liam said. "Welcome to the club."

Scott listened, fascinated, as Liam told the story about how Russ and the town had rallied to save him from an abusive ex when he accidentally found himself stranded nearby with car trouble.

"Whether you're born here, rescued here, or moved here, once you're in Fox Hollow, you belong." Liam laid a hand on Scott's undamaged shoulder before moving through the crowd to find Russ.

First Responder Night was a success, but Squirrel Appreciation Night broke all records. Madden spread the word to the squirrel shifters who had helped defeat the coyotes, and they packed the taproom.

"What about the ones who weren't shifters?" Scott asked Madden. "Can I make a contribution for winter feeding stations or something? They saved my ass."

"Good idea," Madden replied. "Let me see what I can organize. Elias and I can do an event through the comics store and see if we can double or triple your donation."

Scott looked out over the packed bar. "People seem to be having a good time."

"That's because squirrels just want to have fun," Madden said with a grin. "Wait for karaoke."

The DJ had been given a playlist, and as the crowd sang along, it was clear that every song replaced the word girl with squirrel.

Scott hung out at the bar with Gage, and he couldn't remember ever laughing so hard.

"I guess it's true what they say about hard-rockin' squirrels," Scott laughed.

When the night finished and the last patrons wandered outside, Liam was thrilled by the amount raised for the library;

the karaoke DJ had gone through most of his repertoire, and the bar had done a very good business.

Gage refused to let Scott help with the cleanup. He and his barbacks had things sorted quickly, and they all headed out into the evening together. They waved goodnight to the others and headed back to Gage's cabin.

"I'll drive back to Albany with you, and we can rent a truck to move your things," Gage said as they walked into the house. Midnight had come and gone but they were both still stoked from the energy at the bar.

"SPAM set me up in a corporate apartment until I got settled, so I don't have a lease to break. I'll still need to go back to Albany from time to time for more training," Scott replied. "Which means other than a few groceries, I'm not leaving with more than I arrived with. It'll be nice to have company on the drive."

"We can start with what I've got in the cabin and add to it when we see what else we need once you move in," Gage said. "I'm excited to make this place feel like ours."

Scott felt tired but happy as they crawled into bed in the wee hours. They made out for a few minutes, not really intending for it to go anywhere, just for the sake of contact.

"I promise you a very happy wake-up," Scott told Gage as they lay down together. "We're mates. You're my forever guy."

"I could get used to that," Gage murmured, giving Scott a long, lingering press of lips. "I'm counting on it." Scott pressed in for another kiss.

AFTERWORD

A Taste of Danger is part of the Subparheroes series, so be sure you check out all the other books by awesome authors!

All my series as Morgan Brice cross over with each other and with the modern-day series I write as Gail Z. Martin. In this case, the dark witch and his disciples come from my Witchbane series and were killed by Seth and Evan, the main characters of that series, in *Signs and Wonders*.

Fox Hollow is home to its own series of shifters and psychics with plenty of recurring characters. Liam and Russ meet in Huntsman. Austin and Jamie are featured in Haven. Madden and Elias get together in Nutty for You. Brandon finds love in Silent Partner. Noah and Drew connect in Again. Stay tuned for more adventures.

It's a big paranormal world out there!

ACKNOWLEDGMENTS

It really does take a village to bring a book to life. Thank you to all my ARC readers, to my amazing editor, Misty Massey, and to my husband, Larry N. Martin who works so hard behind the scenes to get the books into final form. I couldn't make this happen without you.

Thanks also to the bloggers, assistants, and promotional partners who help spread the word so people know the books exist. I appreciate everything you do.

Most of all, thanks to my wonderful readers, who enjoy visiting and re-visiting the supernatural worlds I write about. You make it all worthwhile. Because you read, I write.

ABOUT THE AUTHOR

Morgan Brice is the romance pen name of bestselling author Gail Z. Martin. Morgan writes urban fantasy male/male paranormal romance, with plenty of action, adventure, and supernatural thrills to go with the happily ever after.

Gail writes epic fantasy and urban fantasy, and together with co-author hubby Larry N. Martin, steampunk and comedic horror, all of which have less romance and more explosions.

On the rare occasions Morgan isn't writing, she's either reading, cooking, or spoiling two very pampered dogs.

Watch for additional new series from Morgan Brice and more books in the Witchbane, Badlands, Treasure Trail, Kings of the Mountain, Sharps & Springfield, and Fox Hollow universes coming soon!

Where to find me, and how to stay in touch

Join my Worlds of Morgan Brice Facebook Group and get in on all the behind-the-scenes fun! My free reader group is the first to see cover reveals, learn tidbits about works-in-progress, have fun with exclusive contests and giveaways, find out about in-person get-togethers, and more! It's also where I find my beta readers, ARC readers, and launch team! Come join the party! https://www.Facebook.com/groups/WorldsOfMorganBrice

Find me on the web at https://morganbrice.com. You can also find me on Twitter/X: @MorganBriceBook, on Pinterest (for Morgan and Gail): pinterest.com/Gzmartin, on Instagram as MorganBriceAuthor, on YouTube at https://www.youtube.com/

c/GailZMartinAuthor/ on Bookbub https://www.bookbub.com/authors/morgan-brice and on TikTok @Morgan-BriceAuthor

Check out the ongoing, online convention ConTinual www.-facebook.com/groups/ConTinual

Support Indie Authors

When you support independent authors, you help influence what kind of books you'll see and what types of stories will be available because the authors themselves decide what to write, not a big publishing conglomerate. Independent authors are local creators supporting their families with the books they produce. Thank you for supporting independent authors and small press fiction!

ALSO BY MORGAN BRICE

Badlands Series

Badlands

Restless Nights, a Badlands Short Story

Lucky Town, a Badlands Novella

The Rising

Cover Me, a Badlands Short Story

Loose Ends

Leap of Faith, A Badlands/Witchbane Novella

Night, a Badlands Short Story

No Surrender

Warm You Up, a Badlands Short Story

Point Blank

Memory and Malice, a Badlands Novella

Shine Tonight, a Badlands Short Story

Fox Hollow Zodiac Series

Huntsman

Again

Silent Partner

Fox Hollow Universe

Romp

Nutty for You

Imaginary Lover

Haven

Gruff

Trash and Treasure

A Taste of Danger: Subparheroes

Kings of the Mountain Series

Kings of the Mountain

The Christmas Spirit, a Kings of the Mountain Short Story

Sins of the Fathers

Kings of the Mountain Universe

Roustabout : Carnival of Mysteries

Sharps & Springfield Series

Peacemaker

Treasure Trail Series

Treasure Trail

Blink

Last Resort

Secrets and Ciphers, a Treasure Trail Novella

Treasure Trail Universe

Light My Way Home, a Treasure Trail Short Story

Witchbane Series

Witchbane

Burn, a Witchbane Novella

Dark Rivers

Flame and Ash

Unholy

The Devil You Know

Signs and Wonders

The Christmas Crunch, a Witchbane Short Story

Sandwiched, a Witchbane Short Story

Ambushed, A Witchbane Novella

Midnight on the Midway: Carnival of Mysteries

Castle Magic: A Caynham Castle Collection

SUBPARHEROES SERIES

9 781647 950729